London's Calling

Nick NiBBs

[INTRO]

For as long as I can remember, alcohol has always been there, like the sun in the sky, only a lot closer, with more appearances. The news, when someone had discovered another shop willing to serve the under-aged, passed through the corridors of my all boys institute quicker than rumours of a new female teacher. Weekend evenings fashioned into sipping bottles of something colourful and low on proof. Spinning around in a field amongst friends whilst parents were in a pub spending the electric bill money. Good old knees up, pints and punches, Dutch courage, love syrup, truth serum, the philosophical sauce. Or, in reality of course, just dumb-minded and distracted.

I didn't really enjoy school as a teen. The snot nose days when learning to read and write was broken up by chasing friends and laughing for no reason, drawing pictures of the family with arms sticking out their heads, and ending in a bean bag with a carton of milk. The sweet voice of a replica Miss Honey would carry me off into an afternoon nap. I'd wake to an empty room with her gently telling me it was time to go home. But the teen school, with a child-sized suit and a rucksack so big and heavy I'd fall onto my back every time I looked up, was something I was quickly bored of. A time divided by running away from the older kids, drawing pictures of atoms that were more confusing than my placement of arms on family portraits, and cartons of milk swapped for sugar rushes. I battled with understanding the motive of being forced to wake just to intake the sum of human knowledge in just five years whilst being half asleep. There were sports, which I enjoyed. Not because I was good at them but because it was more fun kicking or throwing a ball in an open fresh space than it was learning how aggressive the Germans once were in one room, then learning how to order a coffee in their language in the next room.

The importance of doing something you enjoyed was never the pitch. It seemed to be focused on the thing you were likely to succeed most in. In my case, having a lack of focus, it meant nothing. I had to make my own fun there. That included making the passionate historian boil by asking how he knew everything really happened if he wasn't there. And the mathematician to provide a good example in life where one would need to use X to solve a problem. After five years I walked away remembering one word of a foreign language, absolutely nothing from algebra and that the Galea, a Romans soldier's helmet with the red brush, was "used" by the soldiers to clean their uniforms and horses after a long day thrashing spears through the necks of the enemy. Google, when can I start, right?

That said, I wasn't quite ready to stack shelves. That could be my something to fall back on. So I spent another two years improving what was needed to go on to university, where a creative writing course was waiting. This seemed logical to me as it was something I enjoyed doing, something I put my focus into at school to avoid looking at a Bunsen burner and pie charts. I don't remember when exactly I started writing, although I do remember reading comics at night under my bed cover with a torch, which may have inspired me, who knows. But what I did know is that it felt better to write short stories during classes than intake un-useful truths. The thing is, I never actually finished any stories; I would tend to get bored, then dream, just as I would at school, moving on to write something new.

University consisted of drinking during the week and recovering most weekends for three years. After which I went on to work for myself by scooping out and offering my words for free to small businesses and their websites to help build a portfolio from which I might eventually earn a living. It turned out to be fine most of the time, until time itself finally caught up on me, and the need to pay for things became harder to avoid. It became apparent that everything prior did not help me prepare for the next step, the factual world. Drawing my family's arms out from their heads didn't help me with algebra. Algebra didn't help me with writing, and writing didn't help with any business etiquette needed to pay the bills. It almost seemed like once I had moved up in something I was right back at the bottom, learning something else. The only thing I had mastered was the early mornings and the time for when I could eat.

I became very much used to a world where I felt forced to live out a repetitive routine, where not much would happen within a week. Fuelled by hope, it was somewhat more bearable than the continuous search for love and short-lived, sun-seeking getaways. I would constantly find myself standing on the edge of a roof to an unfamiliar building, overlooking a familiar city, one that shares the all too familiar quality - it never sleeps. The empty night sky acted as an oversized cape, wrapping around me and holding down my intoxicated stance as I looked out to a landscape view outlining the infamous structure of the city. Decorated with countless white lights, as if the stars had fallen. I would look down and see only thick blackness, making it impossible to calculate the height, although the pure silence provided loud evidence that I was far from life, therefore close to death.

My favourite song would then begin to play. Tracy Chapman's "Fast Car". I say it's my favourite because I could always listen and sing if I was down or up. That particular song reaches into your emotions, helps comfort sadness and heighten happiness. Once the song replaced the silence, causing my head to rise, I'd begin to watch the dotted lights glow at a slow, smooth pace, in time with the soothing strings of her guitar. Some shone brighter than others. Taking turns before eventually some would fade completely, leaving the survivors to present dot to dot-like visuals. A miraculous show that climaxed with the lights fading away, the cape exhibiting a thicker blackness, where not even my hands could be seen. But this particular week was different. I came across an opportunity from my monotonous life, a chance to escape the trapped-like blueprint that allowed me to have a taste of something you would only find listed on a mythical menu. And I would say it was certainly the pudding to this legendary menu, a discreet and new identity and best of all free alcohol. I guess you could call that the cherry on top. Or if you are not one for drinking whilst working, you could just say it was getting to have some pretty good times, as well as getting paid handsomely for them.

I should slow down a bit before I come off track. Or before I come across as some kind of drunk, deranged hippie, which I'm not. Not that I have anything against hippies whatsoever. If anything, I wish I was more like one. I actually find hippies somewhat; shit there I go.... Let me just start from the very beginning.

[1]

The phone alarm beeped. I dragged myself over towards the siren that's more disturbing than the four-minute warning. The siren that's more disturbing than the four-minute warning. More disturbing than the four-minute warning. THE FOUR-MINUTE WARNING. That robotic baby cry. It creeps inside your head, rattling your skull until your brain wakes where you then sometimes can't help but wish it didn't. I hit the off button and rolled onto my back and stared at the ceiling. In those few minutes, identity and memories pieced together.

Once in the bathroom, I showered and shined my teeth. Feeling a little freshened I half-dressed with the usual two to three minutes looking for my shirt. It was always in the same place, the kitchen, hanging up all creased where the intentions to iron it the night before always end the fridge. I had a shot of vodka, a bit of Dutch encouragement, in preparation for another Monday morning where the main topic of conversation was about the weather, or what I did at the weekend, and what my plans were for the next. An absolute on-going, mind-boggling dilemma as to how my work environment was never listed as the eighth wonder of the world. I stood and admired my girlfriend Gabriella, whom I often called Peach, someone I felt should be listed as the eighth wonder. That morning her hair was shaped like an arrow pointing towards half of her bum that hung out from the duvet. I tucked her back in, gave her a subtle kiss on her forehead and headed out.

Me and my creased shirt then waited for a bus where we would soon sit amongst so many more other creased humans and hung-over shirts. It was like a bus full of sick

5

animals en route to the vet. Twenty-three minutes later I arrived at my did-not-really- have-a-choice work place. I stood outside looking up at the building for a moment, glaring, eager the dull worn bricks would change to something brighter. Just looking for any evidence of warmth I felt was needed for a place I spent more time in than home. But it never changed. I scratched my head and took a deep breath before approaching the main doors, which also needed replacing. They seemed more fed-up than I did. Each time you pulled one it would stop, get stuck, and you had to tug it three times before it was ajar. Even then you still had to squeeze through. The main reception was always cold and dark, lacking bulbs and natural light where the only thing slightly visible was the lift. It was like flat-lining, except you were making your way towards a vague light. Even death was an effort there. I entered and pushed for the third floor, and then embraced the last few moments of normality before the doors opened to a world where your head would jolt, with every tick of every second from a clock.

The lift reached the third level. The doors began to open slowly but surely, screeching out for some kind of oil, displaying the cramped space. White walls that had become brown, metal gutters dressing the edge of the room that were supposed to hide the wiring. The majority hung out, looking for an escape. And then there were the squared ceiling tiles where every other one was missing or broken in half. That completed the elaborate space. A room of six rows and ten stations split equally by a slim path leading to the toilets, the staff kitchen, and a fifteen-litre water cooler, which never had cups. An eye-sore of fifty-nine computers, twenty-five spectacles and zero hydrated people equipped to sell triple glazing to citizens who couldn't even afford window cleaner. A civilised prison, my cell was on the third row, where to my right was a young girl called Sophie Pain, who, despite her family name, actually eased some of the hurt in going in. She wasn't as quiet as the brown wall to my left but she was quiet nonetheless and very sweet. Sophie rarely came out for drinks but when she did she would spend most of the night dancing with a huge smile on her face, always making a sensible early departure. She was smart, focused and full of hope.

"Good morning."

"Morning Sophie."

"How are you?"

"Not too bad thank you, yourself?"

"I'm fine. Freezing this morning, wasn't it?"

I presented a frown and a subtle smirk. Sophie would soon notice the lack of my reply.

"What?" she replied with a questioning gape.

"Nothing. Yes, it was. It was horrible."

Sophie then picked up a Tupperware full of cookies and held it out to me.

"Chocolate chip with extra melted milk chocolate."

"My favourite."

"I know."

"You're very sweet Sophie, thank you."

"Welcome."

I sat enjoying my favourite freshly made cookie only to be interrupted by a worn-down, coffee filled Bonner.

"Fifty-nine people logged on out of sixty, can you guess who the one is?"

"Hi Tim."

"Mr Bonner," he said firmly.

Yes, my boss was called *Mr*. Bonner and insisted you called him that. Unlike Sophie, he asserted his family name into his personality, or at least tried to maintain a hard warden like presence. It didn't quite work, not with me anyway, as I knew him outside the prison, which he always seemed to forget. Or maybe him knowing parts of me, he thought I would forget. Who knew.

"Fifty-nine people logged on out of sixty; can you guess who the one is?" Bonner repeated, only this time gritting his teeth.

"I'm thinking because you are not at your computer that it's you?"

"Wrong it's you, and not the first time this month. In fact, you are leading that target by quite a sufficient amount. I'm sure if Sophie weren't feeding you cookies you would have logged on by now."

"Actually, I took the cookie from her. She was working before I arrived."

"Right. Well, hurry up and finish it, then join me in my office."

"What for?"

"I need to speak with you."

"Ok."

Bonner then moved his focus onto Sophie. I watched him work his magic, just like we were at a bar on a Thursday after work.

"So what cookies have you made today Sid?"

"What?" a baffled Sophie replied.

"Sid. Sesame Street. The cookie monster!"

"Oh, I don't know what that means, sorry."

Sophie looked over at me and then faced her computer screen. I caught an awkward Bonner looking at me and I raised my eyebrows whilst nibbling into my cookie.

"Very well. Ok, I shall be in my office," Bonner continued whilst pointing at me.

Bonner walked away with his tail between his legs. I continued to pick out the chocolate chunks in my tasty treat, eating them one by one.

"What do you think he wants?" Sophie gossiped over to me.

"Huh?"

"What do you think he wants to see you for?"

"Oh, I don't know. Probably to tell me how wonderful his weekend was and all the imaginary phone numbers he got."

"Did you not go out?"

"No. Taking a break."

"I bet Gabby likes that."

"Maybe."

I never let a Bonner get in my way before, and I wasn't going to start then. I finished my cookie before getting up and making my way to the toilet. The toilet was always my go-to when I needed a break. It contained two cubicles, always lacked soap and had an old rusty towel machine on the wall. The one where you would have to pull the towel down and roll it around to get an untouched piece of cloth. It never had any material in it; it was useless but not completely, as I used it to stash a flask containing some smooth aged brandy to help get me through the day. When I went to retrieve it, it was no longer there. I assumed the cleaner, who visited the building once every six months, must had finally found it. And, being that I was expected in the office, a toilet nap was out of the question. With nothing else to do, I took a deep breath and made my way down to the Bonner.

"Mr late log on, take a seat."

I took a battered chair from the corner of a boxed room and sat opposite Bonner. He held a few sheets of paper and a pen whilst leaning on his plastic desk, acting as the godfather but looking more like an Au pair in a toddler play den.

"So what did you get up to on the weekend?" he said, a glaring smile held on his face.

And Monday's matinee had begun. The same play, different stage scenario, where I decided to take the spontaneous understudy role.

"I actually went to Paris."

"With gabby?"

"Nope. On my own. I wanted something chilled but it led to a night in the city where a strange but friendly Frenchman took me to a high-end gentleman's club. He got me in for free and I ended up going back with the Madame, and well. Let's just say she was very hungry and I happened to have a baguette on me."

"Really?"

"No, I stayed in with Gabby, like I told you I was doing when you messaged me seventeen times."

"You should have come out. The girls were phenomenal."

"I promised gabby I wouldn't go out for a while."

"That's shitty."

"It's necessary."

"For who?"

"I don't know, for us."

"I was on fire, I got like twelve numbers."

"Awesome."

"There was one you would have loved. I was trying to take a picture of her to send to you but I lost her when she went into the toilet."

"Please don't send me pictures. And why are you following girls to the toilets?"

"I was trying to get you out."

"I was with Gabby, plus, when have I ever gone out for the girls?"

"What do you mean?"

"I go out for the alcohol, nothing else."

"Oh. Well, I'm out for the girls. And speaking of alcohol do you happen to know anything about this?"

He took out my brandy flask and placed it softly onto the plastic desk with a few magicians' flicks from his fingertips, like he was some kind of smooth detective who'd had just discovered vital evidence to a big case. Again, trying to separate business and pleasure, which I always found strange. I mean, I'd seen the man shovel white powder up his nose several times in one sitting whilst griping me in excitement. The excitement caused by the female company I would acquire through friendly and open conversation. I've even felt the sweat from his nose fall onto my hand, and I've witnessed him cry after repeating the same crude jokes to women, thinking it would somehow excite them. They say you can't blame a man for trying, but I've seen that there is plenty of blame to go around, and Bonner got the majority. And for some reason, we had to sit there when he chose, pretending like none of that happened. He wasn't a friend, exactly, just merely a person who knew bits of my life without knowing a thing about how I felt.

"Yeah, it's mine."

Bonner sat staring with a shocked expression on his face.

"I know that, but you're not meant to say... I have to report it now."

"Why?"

"Because drinking during work hours is against the code of conduct. This is not the first time and I feel it's because you don't want to be here."

How he thought anyone would want to be there was amazing. The best and sole thing that ever came from the place was meeting Gabby. I remember seeing her for the first time in the staff kitchen. The good thing about moments is you can always go back to them, a scrapbook of memories where you control what to watch.

"Gabriella right?"
"Yes. Hello."
"How are you finding it here?"
"Boring."
"I would like to say you get used to it, but you don't."
"I won't be here long. It's just temporary until September."
"Studying?"
"Yes."
"What will you be studying?"
"Nursing."
"That's nice."
"Would you like a peach?"

She held out a carton of peaches with one remaining peach inside.

"Thank you. Did you eat the whole carton?"
"I love them. They are not as fresh as I'm used to but they are my favourite fruit. I grew up on a peach farm with my grandparents."
"That sounds fun."
"It was."
"Where are you from?"
"Cenes de la vega. Spain. South. Close to Granada."
"I haven't been."
"You should, it's beautiful."
"Maybe I will. Maybe we can go together and you can show me around."
"Maybe." Glancing over at me and smiling.
Her face was nice to look at and her smile always made my day.
"And maybe you can show me London," she said faintly whilst turning away.
"Anytime."

14

I could see us staring into one another's eyes and could feel the rush like I was there, in a room I wanted to be in, with a person I wanted to be with. The bad thing about moments is you can always get dragged back into reality.

"Anytime? What? Are you even listening to me?"

And I was back sitting in a room I didn't want to be in, with a person I didn't want to be with.

"Sorry, what did you say?"

"I said I would have to arrange a meeting to discuss disciplinary action."

"That sounds like too much effort. I will just quit instead."

"You can't just quit. You need to hand in a notice."

"No I don't. I just need to walk out the door."

I stood up and took a deep breath whilst stretching my arms up.

"What will Gabby think?"

"Ahhh. One-step forward two steps back, it's what she loves about me."

"Do you know what I love about you?"

I shook my head as I felt that would be somewhat subliminal. I didn't care for words. But you would have more luck in a plane plummeting to the ground and stepping out of it without a scratch than you would stop

15

Bonner from speaking. And that's without any class A drug in his system.

"I love how you can have a little but seem like you have a lot. Well, the old you could anyway. I don't think this new guy will cope."

"Maybe."

I rapidly left the room and headed back to my cell to say goodbye to Sophie.

"Sophie! Stand up."

"What?"

"Quickly, stand up."

A worried confused Sophie stood and I gave her a squeeze.

"What happened?" she concernedly asked.

"I quit. I'm going home."

"Why?"

"Because Sophie, there's no place like it. Take care and keep dancing."

I walked away and was immediately interrupted by the sweetness that was Sophie Pain, touching my shoulder and holding out her Tupperware pot.

"Here take them."

"All of them?"

"Yep."

"Thank you Sophie."

"Welcome."

So as a less worried but more confused Sophie began sitting back down, I walked away feeling the warmth which that building never provided before, excited to go back to something even warmer. I waited freely at the bus stop, lit up a cigarette along with the comforting thought of cuddling up with Gabby, and naturally give her a heads up to encourage her to stay put.

[Text message]
To: Peach
I'm on my way back xx

[Text message]
From: Peach
Why?

[Text message]
To: Peach
I got fired xx

[Text message]
From: Soft Bonner
Drinks this week?

[2]

I sat on the bus again, this time amongst only creased humans. Pensioners starting off the day slightly after the rest, with their morning bus ride to the supermarket for the week's lottery, followed by the bingo hall or pub; the good old life. Before home, I stopped at a nearby supermarket to grab Gabby some peaches, hoping it would avoid any tension. I took my keys out, opened the door and entered cautiously. I placed Sarah's Tupperware pot down in the kitchen and made my way toward the bedroom, still holding the cartoon of peaches. But it seemed not even a peach tree would have been of interest. I noticed my personal belongings on the floor looking so happy to see me, only the feeling wasn't mutual. Such a sight is not a world wonder. The only thing I could have been grateful for was that my heads up text message was encouraged, even if it wasn't to my satisfaction. With little, but enough, pride left inside I approached a giant curled up peach on the bed and touched her shoulder.

"Hi?"

The first dagger to the heart. Complete silence.

"It will be ok Gabby."

"What happened?" she asked, with a bulging frown on her face.

"I just wasn't keeping up with targets."

"Mentiroso."

18

The fact she called me a liar in Spanish was a clear tell that she was not upset, she was angry. I knew then that it was only a matter of seconds before the second dagger would be flying my way.

"I rang Tim and he said you had been drinking again at work. He found a flask?"

"It wasn't mine."

"Mentiroso!"

"It's not like I can't go back or find something similar, I just don't want to be there."

"Why didn't you just say that?"

"Say what?"

"That you didn't want to be there instead of drinking yourself to get through the day and denying things all the time."

"I didn't want you to worry."

"I can't do this right now. The stress is not good for the baby."

"I know that, which is why.."

"I want to have a break!" Interrupting me.

"What?"

"I packed your things for you."

19

"I noticed, thank you, and I got you some peaches so it's good we're thinking of each other."

"Please just go, mentiroso."

I should have left it, but I couldn't.

"I'm not a liar."

She pounced on me like a Latin lion, me a baby gazelle with three legs, drowning amongst a crocodile-infested lake. She began climbing on me over and over with both arms whilst projecting deep roars and fearful tears as I tried to dodge her powerful jaws. I eventually escaped and left, thankful that I got to live another day. And so with the power of amateur dramatics and the repetition of *basura* still playing over in my head, which means trash, I left the apartment carrying my belongings, all so fittingly chucked into black bin bags. It was the slow torturous trip that would lead me to holding a bottle of something strong, awaiting the sun to appear through the darken, ugly clouds resembling a breakup.

[3]

It seemed sensible to go visit the one person who had been through it before. The very man who told me the tale of the young and old bull.

One day a young bull and an old bull were taking a stroll; soft grass massaged their hooves whilst a hard sun touched their heads. The younger bull noticing a field of cows, excitedly spilled out, "quick let's run down and flirt with a few," where the older bull replied, "no let's walk down and flirt with all of them."

A person who would have no reason to lie or even sugar coat something; I preferred it that way, the telling-it-how-it-is approach.

Times may change but the idea of a life will certainly not. - Someone. Once

The apartment door was always unlocked. I was never too sure if it was simply down to the fact that he didn't have to remember his keys if he popped out, or if he was just living in the past, where he was used to leaving the door open during the warming seasons, when someone breaking in was just unheard of. I entered the man cave and was greeted by the clutter. More wood than the local forest, old electronics that never even worked properly when they were new. The dated music, mixed with the familiar smell of overcooked food, rekindled my senses and I suddenly became eight years old again.

"And what do I owe the pleasure?" The words softly emerging from within the sofa, along with a cloud of smoke.

I sat opposite him, placed my bin bags down and took out a fresh can of beer from the corner shop.

After a big gulp, I lit up a cigarette and contributed to the smoke storm.

"I just had some free time, thought I'd check in." I mumbled, throat full of nicotine.

"Are you working?"

"No. I got fired."

He chuckled and sat up.

"Gabby's pregnant. She kicked me out."

Another chuckle, this time a deeper tone, formed from the depths of life experience. A few moments of silence followed, the usual intake of my emotions absorbed through squinting eyes whilst the cigarette shortened and the cryptic dialogue was being analysed within his mind. An expected tale would follow, then a monologue of sorts, and then ending again with the tale and a change of subject, focusing on me.

"You can lie to yourself, you can lie to others but you can't lie to the universe."

"OK," I replied whilst taking another gulp of patience.

"Everyone thinks they are special. Can change the world, do it better than those previous. In order to do that you need notice the choices before you're even in the situation. Everything we do, what makes us, is all formed from memory. Even the things you can't remember, they are still there in you. Being born and being held we don't remember, experiencing unconditional love before our eyes are even open, stays in us, most of us. Trauma builds, simply from the repetition and idea of something as opposed to the reality. You and Gabby are both from broken families, meaning you both have an idea in your head of how things should be, a constant battle. As a man you will lose. You have to see it from the other side; it's hard but it is necessary. Losing your job doesn't exactly portray stability or security to a woman and that is all that matters now."

"I can get another job."

Another chuckle, that time with a clicking noise bouncing between his cheeks, followed by a large exhale of breath.

"Even a horse can see you are not ready."

"I think I'm ready."

"Really? What do you think a good dad is?"

"I don't know. Just being there?"

"You think you even have that choice? Everyone thinks the same. Playing catch, just being there. How are you going to do that as well as earn money, when you don't even have a job? I lost my job just before you were born so the worries weren't there, but it didn't take long after the worries and problems came. I spent two years with you everyday until the divorce. After I didn't see you, I would drink that shit you have in your hand every night, sometimes hoping I wouldn't wake up because being with you everyday for two years to then not knowing when I would see you again was taking its toll. Then I would be happy to wake because it meant I could see you. Experiencing the only part of hope you have left is used to invite death. Cancer or any kind of harm is no longer feared but welcomed. You think that's how I thought it would be? Are you ready for that? No matter how special you think you are, if you are showing you don't even care about your own health, then why would anyone think you care about someone else's. You can lie to yourself and to others, but you can't lie to the universe."

"What does that even mean?"

"It means many things. Mainly if you put in genuine effort and know yourself, even if others don't agree, the universe will reward you with what you truly deserve. Many things are fake. The efforts, the lifestyle, more so today, are portrayed as genuine but the reward and emotions are not. Because the universe won't reward that. It may for a short while or even a long period, with money or "success". But the simple truths and desires you want, well, eventually the shine will fade. For now all you can do is try to show your support, show you are not going anywhere."

"I will."

"There are two different jobs now; to be a father and a partner. Most struggle with one. In order to separate that you still need to do something for yourself, to express and release. That's why art is good - someone may or may not like what you do but there's no right or wrong, its an extension of you, which you need to find before you can extend another life. Art is grey, just like the world we live in. The more you practice the more you will see. Are you still writing?"

"Sometimes."

"Good. But for now that means putting aside your own dreams, make some money somewhere, somehow."

"I will."

"Do you need to stay here?"

"No I will stay at Madhav's old place."

"How is Madhav, still backdoor selling?"

"Yeah, of course he is."

"Such a dark horse that kid."

"Ok, I have to go."

"All righty, until next time."

I stopped at an off licence and purchased a few more cans to slow down my thoughts before checking into a cheap hotel I was familiar with. In the un-cleaned box-room, I pulled the dust-filled curtains to darken my surroundings, then sat in the corner of the room and began sipping I must have nodded off because I woke thirty-seven minutes later, deciding the best thing to do was get organised. I hung my clothes in a broken wardrobe and arranged my toiletries in order of use on a shelf. I wasn't quite sure what to do after that, so the easiest thing seemed to continue sipping, along with some daytime television. The risk here was to be bombarded with dozens of reality shows and third world advertising all feeding demoralised lifestyles in the hope that one would feel some form of gratitude. The choice of alcohol wasn't complementing the mood either. The reoccurrences had made my sorrows too strong a swimmer, exempt from drowning, doing nothing but throw them a party. A quarter or so through the third can it kicked, and I started to feel like joining in, getting out to take my mind away from it all. I began to message friends, enquiring about their plans for the evening. Halfway through the bottle, and halfway through the TV guide, it wasn't long after I had hooked someone. Naturally, I showered and shined my teeth before changing into my lucky shirt. One that was suitable but too good for work, as it never creased to amaze me.

I took a few last sips and made my way to the train station to meet my pal, Paul. Paul and I grew up together, a school friend. The kind of friend you don't see regularly but nothing has changed when you do, apart from the fact he had a testicle removed. And despite the expected lower testosterone levels he had become a lot testier and was always finding trouble, or trouble was finding him. Who knew.

[4]

Myself and Paul stepped off underground and made our way to street level where I became conscious of my dejected mood. It seemed natural, given the circumstances, but it was heavier than usual. Much like the shower that was crashing down from the ugly dark cloud which had followed me out. Standing sheltered for a moment in the exit, Paul front line, we planned our route of attack to the first pub, watching the thick rain bounce off the floor. The appreciation of the smell of water that fell from a hosed down hedge onto heated paved stones during the summer was all forgotten. It was more like the world was tipped upside down, spilling out the river Thames on top of me. Thick grumpy drops, so large they reflected my glum expression, and the murky classic modern war field of construction that surrounded us.

Good old London. A town where everyone is in a rush to go nowhere, partaking in the everlasting race no one actually gets to win. Dragging ourselves from bed each morning and grouping like rats underground, hoping for that piece of cheese we were promised if we worked hard enough. Energizing our bodies with caffeine in order to get through the week. Then the weekend binge, sinking our brains in drugs and alcohol in order to forget the week before, week after week, year after year, corroding our souls until the time we find ourselves slouched in the corner of a room, surrounded by family, hearing the grandchildren ask: what's wrong with Grandpa? To which we say: he's just old kids, protecting them with a lie instead of preparing them with the truth – being that we all live in hope of the day we will be free to sleep, wake, go where we please. Although that day only comes when we

27

can no longer pull a Christmas cracker or lift our arse up to fart. I was miserable. I could only be thankful that I had quit my job, as that meant it wouldn't be a night where having to go to work the next day slapped the smile from your face every time you began to let loose.

It wasn't long before we made our charge and reached first base. Ordering a shot we asked the barman to choose for us, along with a pint of beer to wash it down. We then found an empty table and set up camp.

[BAR 1 9:15 PM]

"Cheers," Paul said, with a plain expression on his face.

"Cheers."

We touched glasses and had a sip of beer, picked up our surprise shot, touched glasses and took them down.

"So, how is everything?" I went first.

"Same old crap, working my arse off."

"Anything new?"

"Just took on a large contract actually. Going pretty well."

"That's good."

"Yeah. Just busy."

"How's Emma?"

"We broke up."

28

"You're kidding?"

"Lastttt Thursday, yeah Thursday. Haven't heard a dicky bird since."

"What do you mean? Where is she?"

"She's at the house, I'm staying at my brother's."

"Oh."

"Yep."

So it seemed that Paul was also a freshly wounded soldier from the war of romance. Although with Paul and Emma it was more surprising. I'd only been with Gabby for three years and they had earned the decade badge. Paul was hard work. Always was a loveable and caring fellow, just a little difficult to tame. In his early years of two testicles, he would always go missing. He loved to be around celebrations or big events. He'd go out alone to sniff out birthdays and weddings; eves drop a few names and act as a relative or friend and hover amongst the group. He even booked to watch the 2014 World Cup Final in Germany, and when they won he claimed his father's side was German and just followed the parties for a whole week. It never seemed to affect the relationship as Emma just made use of the time to get on with her career in the city, and although I had never met her she seemed to be his anchor. Without her, Paul would always sail towards high waves and lightning-filled skies.

"How are you and gabby?"

"Nope."

"What happened?"

"I lost my job and she wasn't best pleased that we didn't discuss it."

"Fucksake. I'm off tomorrow. Let's have a good night. I'm getting us another shot."

And right then it turned into the traditional breakup crawl. That consisted of hitting three or four places before making it to a dark, overcrowded, overpriced spot where we would reach a drunken level that unleashes the language only equivalent crawlers know. A place where usually a game of hide and seek unravels and you spend most of the night circling and looking for that familiar face before giving up and dancing alone, holding a warm bottle of beer while giving a paralytic dance performance, like a giraffe trying to walk after being born, adding to the many aches the following morning.

[BAR 2 9:59 PM]

After our other shot in first base, which turned out to be three tequilas each, we moved on to a cocktail bar, just catching the last order for happy hour, making Paul extremely cheerful. So much so he didn't bother to comment on the many groups of single ladies that packed out the place, at least not until we had found a table.

"Yes, yes, yes, definitely, yes, don't like what she is wearing but yes, she looks a bit like a cousin.... still would."

The waitress then brought us six cocktails. Paul did try and haggle more but he came to a compromise with the manager, owing to the offer being about to finish. So we sat side by side with six pina Coladas and two more tequilas for a good ten minutes without saying a word to one another. The music caught Paul's ears and he slowly bopped his head whilst twiddling his cocktail umbrella, sipping through his pink straw before he continued his victim role.

"Listen to this then."

"Go on?"

"You know I brought Emma that puppy?"

"Bought. Yeah?"

"She doesn't even take it out. I come home and have to walk it. Remember to feed it in the morning before work, pick up its shit."

"What dog is it?"

"One of them mixed miniature poodle, noodle, I don't know."

"Well, she must be doing all that now?"

"No, the fucker's staying with me. She packed a bag for it and everything. My brother has two pythons and they're refusing to eat the mice and he thinks it's because of the dog. I'm at work stressing about them smashing through the tank and eating the dog."

"Hahahaha."

"I can't stand her snobby work friends. She wants me to go to these dinners and honestly, I'd rather starve. They all sit there sipping wine with their pinkies sticking up, airing them out from being stuck up their arses."

"Just tell her it's not for you and the two of you just go out."

"I'm too busy to even think about planning a night out. And if I do she'll be working late, and if she plans something I'm working late. Ah I don't know."

"Well, imagine if you had a kid?"

"What do you mean?"

"If you're struggling to spend time now because of work, do you really think trying for a kid is the right thing?"

"It will be different. We won't work as much. She wants a baby badly. And to be honest I do too. We just haven't had any luck because of this fucking ball-shit."

Paul hit his lap with force three times.

"Have you been tested since the operation?"

"Of course, I'm at the hospital more than the doctors. They said everything is fine, just a lower chance. I just didn't expect it to be this low. Honestly, some weeks I feel drier than this."

He picked up the dried slice of pineapple from his cocktail.

I didn't mention to Paul that Gabby was pregnant. It didn't seem right. There I was being in a two-year relationship with Gabby who was taking medication to block any chances of us conceiving. Yet we had, and Paul was at it twice a day for years, had made charts and graphs, visits to the doctors, but he couldn't even swim past the half way mark. I know he would have been pleased for me but I also knew it would only remind him that he couldn't have the one thing he wanted.

"Come on let's get out of here." He said whilst standing.

We finished our cocktails and continued our quest to the next bar. Paul had caught the jitterbug and wanted to hear some louder music, so naturally we moved on to a place with live music.

[BAR 3 11:20 PM]

We managed to find an event where, despite a ticket only entry, Paul managed to get us in. Confidently convincing the security that his cousin "Ian" was playing in one of the bands, we just walked right in. Finding a table toward the back away from the stage, we were approached by a waiter.

"What do you want?" A heavy-eyed Paul said whilst slanted and looking over at me.

"Anything. Same as you."

"Double whisky please, two."

We sat scoping for while before the waiter delivered our drinks at the same time a performer walked onto the stage. It seemed once again we had got to the bar in

33

perfect time. A stylish laid-back lady in her mid-twenties holding a guitar began adjusting her seat and microphone. I could already hear her voice. And I just knew what she was going to play, my favourite song. When she started the intro the whole bar became silent to me. I couldn't even hear Paul slurping his whisky. I sat back and closed my eyes and began flipping through my scrapbook of moments and chose the third night that I and Gabby had been out when she had invited me back to hers. I'd picked up a framed picture of her and a cat from the table in the living area.

"That was my pet lynx," Gabby said with a soft tone.
"A wild cat?"
"Yes. My granddad found a den and there was a baby."
"How did he know the mum lynx wasn't just getting some food?"
"They were hunted and killed a lot. He knew she wasn't coming back."
"I didn't even know lynx were from Spain."
"Where I was from there were. We looked after it for a few months, so not so much a pet."
"I used to collect snails."
"Snails?"
"Yep. I kept them in a shoebox."
"Hahahaha." She erupted with laughter.
"I had two goldfish, which I overfed and they died, and then a hamster I never fed so that died."
"You couldn't manage a hamster, how old were you?"
"Not sure, six or so."
"Ok, I'll let you off."
"Thank you."
"Do you want a drink? I have some vodka."
"Are you trying to get me drunk?"
"Maybe.

"I already find you attractive chica. I don't need to be drunk."

"Very smooth. Well, maybe it's to help me."

"Ouch."

"I'm joking."

"Plus, I have to drive home."

"Why don't you stay tonight, drive home tomorrow?"

"Ok. Sounds good."

"I don't know what to do," Paul said whilst whimpering.

And I opened my eyes only to see Paul had gone through three more doubles and I was back in a room with an emotionally troubled train wreck.

"What?" I said.

"I just said the wrong words, I think it's a great idea, I'm going to call her."

"No, it will only make things worse. Just give her space. Come on let's go somewhere else."

"I want to see some boobs." Paul whimpered like a kid wanting some sweets.

"OK. I'll take you to see some boobs!"

We left the music venue and didn't have to travel far. There was a strip club just two doors down and we approached it trying to keep our eyes open, and steps balanced. Once we entered, Paul handed over our entry fee to a glamorous receptionist wearing large black glasses at a small desk set just outside the main room. We were patted down by a giant of a man, or rather hit several times from the ankles up before he continued his exhibition of

35

strength, firmly grabbing a large battered suede curtain whilst warning us to keep our phones in our pockets at all times. He then pulled the curtain aside to reveal a box-room without lights, displaying many girls lacking clothes. We watchfully entered, walking cautiously for a moment whilst listening to the loud, distorted music choking the room. Paul headed straight to the bar and scoped the display of whiskies on show. I stood next to him and scoped the display of custom. There were a mixture of groups and even some on their lonesome. The group that stood out was made up of several men, where one stood out above the rest, dressed in a blonde wig and pink dress; the stag of a stag night, I assumed. There was another group of younger guys, front row of the stage watching a topless girl. She was eight foot high up a pole, performing a trick by releasing her grip, sticking out both her arms and throttling her chest, bouncing her breasts. The young lads stared, their heads all bopping simultaneously with her chest. I couldn't watch her anymore; it was nerve racking to see someone that high up without any head and knee protection, but I felt reassured by so many ready to catch her. The room was like an evolutionary relationship chart. With the young single lads, right the way up to the divorced men sitting alone, the stag group in between. Then there were myself and Paul, both in a relationship and single at the same time. A clear moment where no matter where you are in your life, men will continue to surround themselves with the opposite sex until the day they die, or at least the day they lose their sight.

Before any further integration of the room, Paul arguing with the barmaid over the price of the drinks interrupted me. He said it was discriminatory, not to have the price on the menus. Then he accused her of making the prices up. Unfortunately, Paul raised his voice during the transition to the next song, where the music became minimal. It had caught the giant man's ear and the bullying of the suede curtain continued as he appeared, glaring at us like a concerned gorilla. I tapped Paul on the shoulder with some reassuring words and he walked away, swinging his head from side to side whilst giving the barmaid one last look of hatred. Paul transitioned along with the next song and bounced his way ahead of me to a table in the middle of the room. The group of young lads were in front, the stag behind, and two lonesome either side of us. After relaxing our backsides and sipping on some overpriced whisky, two girls approached us. One sat on Paul's lap and the other sat in an empty seat beside me. Paul was already in the cave man state. The intake of alcohol hijacking his brain and kicking out any romantic emotion, he was simply a talking animal looking to reproduce, and I was to witness something spectacular. Something that had taken man thousands of years to master. Putting to shame the sweet songs of any bird call designed to impress their potential mate. Something you would not be able to teach the younger lads. Something the divorcees would give a respectful nod to, admitting they were out of practice. The most seductive magical mating call that no woman could ever resist:

"How much for me to see your stinky pinky?"

Even more seductively, he was literally spitting out his words onto her face.

The girl took Paul by the hand and led him astray to the opposite side of the entrance. A gracefully treated suede curtain was eased aside and they disappeared into a secret part of the building.

"Your friend has a way with words."

The girl beside me spoke up, repositioning her chair, moving closer to me.

"His brain thinks something else, but by the time it gets to his mouth it changes. He was complementing her really. You just need to know him."

"So what brings you here?"

"Him," I replied, whilst pointing over to the last place I saw Paul.

"Have you been here before?"

"No."

"Have you ever had a dance before?"

"I have."

"How was it?"

"It was ok, not really for me if I'm honest."

"Well that's because you haven't had a dance from me."

"Maybe."

"Would you like to go for one?"

"Not right now, I just want to sit with my friend Jack," I said as I held the glass of whisky up.

"Crystal to the stage, Crystal to the stage." An announcement from a hidden male voice ran over the music.

That's me I have to go, she said whilst standing and pulling down her dress.

"Crystal?" I questioned.

"It's a stage name."

"What's your real name?" I asked whilst faintly smiling.

"Sophia. And yours?"

"Boris."

"Boris? You're lying."

"So are you."

She sniggered and walked away. I sipped my drink, enjoying a moment of peace. Crystal reached the stage whilst a new song began playing. Her eyes fixed upon me and I returned the favour for a moment before returning my attention to the drink, swirling the ice cube with my finger. When I finally placed my eyes back onto Crystal, her attention was shared with the front row fresher's.

I felt lost now, although I didn't care to be found. Off track, but unsure as to which direction I should go. Before I could work on my own problems, somebody else's disturbed me. The giant had appeared from behind his curtain and thudded his way over to the second delicate curtain, disappearing for a few seconds before he returned, dragging Paul by the elbow, directing him towards the exit.

Everything had stopped except the music. The youngsters, the stag, the lonesome and even Crystal on stage all watched the spectacle. Crystal then looked over to me, gritting her teeth. I rolled my eyes before standing. She subtly waved at me, and I smiled before waving back. I made it outside, dodging the confrontation with the giant before noticing Paul struggling to stand a few metres away, looking how I felt.

"What did you do?" (I don't know why I asked).

"Nothing, I didn't do anything!" Paul slurred with anger

"You must have done something!"

"She was teasing me, and I was touching her."

"You can't do that."

"You don't know the full story."

"I do know because it's always the same one."

"Why are you on their side?"

"Clearly I'm on their side standing here with you!"

"They're fucking whores, they get touched all the time and then…"

"They're just working, some of them have kids," interrupting him

"Exactly, how the fuck do they have kids and I don't. It's not fair."

"OK. But you can't take it out on other people, it will just go round and round, it's not her fault."

"Why are you sticking up for her she's a ..."

"So why didn't that stop you touching her?" interrupting him once again.

"What?"

"If she's so bad a person, why did you want to touch her?"

"Oh I see. You're all protective because of your mum."

"What's that supposed to mean?"

"Nothing."

"No say it?"

"Let's just go somewhere else."

"I'm going home, you should probably do the same."

"No, I'm staying out."

"OK, well that's the end of this then."

[BAR 4 12:05 AM]

I didn't go home after what seemed to be the final scene, seeing as I was charged twenty-five pounds to enter. Instead, I rushed ahead of the queue in desperate need to empty some of the alcohol to make space for the new

41

batch. I sat at the bar and continued to drink with my back to the many hide and seek games going on behind me. An hour or so in, the overload began to take its toll. The part I like to refer to as 'the drop'. An autopilot state where one minute you can be lifting your glass to your mouth and the next you are in a smoking area talking to a stranger and laughing at a joke you only hear the punch line to. Minutes turn into seconds, seconds into blinks, each one changing the scene and location. Watching a slide show flicking by so fast it moulds the many pictures into one big blur. Mixing laughter with bits of conversation and even smells bypassed the encounters, the slow reflexes of all your senses, which then all come together at once. They speed through your mind until finally your feet, and the sound of a door closing, are the last things you see and hear before, you drop.

[5]

The phone alarmed beeped and I rolled over and hit the off button. Then onto my back, staring at the ceiling whilst the memories and identity pieced together. Suffering from a sleep deficiency, it took longer than usual, the effect of never being fully asleep, and never fully awake. Eventually, my conscious and subconscious marry, and I'm faced with the constant struggle in separating my intentions from my actions, my thoughts from what was said, forever trying to remember my movements, frequently repeating the words.

It all sounds very confusing, which is exactly how it was. It was quite easily the go-to thing I would wish on a worst enemy. I had suffered with it for a while. I first pursued some assistance from sleeping pills I called 'snoozers' and they worked for a couple of months or so, but like most drugs taken often, immunity builds, after which the only thing I found helped replace the snoozers was alcohol itself. The many mornings suffering from the repercussions of a headache in a flaccid body made the nights worthwhile. And even more so when I eventually worked out that continuing to drink, once awake, removed those consequences. It all seemed to be working out until the excess led to another immunity and I found myself right back at the wedding between fantasy and reality, only this time with a plus one. Never fully awake and never fully asleep, accompanied by never fully drunk and never fully sober. Entering a world where the bottom of a bottle became limitless, and my actions became even more difficult to place. My words repeated even more.

After my identity puzzle was put together, I sat up and noticed an unopened can of beer on the floor amongst three empties I must have picked up on my way home. I reached down for the can, opened it and took a few sips to begin eradicating my head and lethargic aches. I then picked up my phone and came across two messages and three missed calls. One message from Paul with the usual:

[Text message]
From: One ball Paul
WherEe rarre yoou??

And then three missed calls from him probably with the same motive. The other message I had received was at 3:26 am.

[Text message]
From: London's Calling
Flick Beans café 12 pm

For the life of me I could not place who this was. I assumed I had made a drunken promise and agreed to meet someone, and hoped it was a drunken arrangement from him or her too. The name saved didn't hint anything either. In fact, it made it more baffling. It's what I tend to do, apply a nickname so it makes it more personal and adds character to my address book, as well as helping me link a memory saved on a drunken night. But "London's Calling" wasn't exactly "Football Fred" or "Guy Who Owns Bar". I put no further force into it and just continued drinking my beer and reversing my headache, whilst checking in on Paul.

[Text message]
To: One ball Paul
What happened to you? What time did you get home?

44

[Text message]
From: One ball Paul
Had an argument with the bouncer no idea 3 am maybe.

[Text message]
To: One ball Paul
What, why?

[Text message]
From: One ball Paul
Said I was too drunk

[Text message]
From: London's Calling
Still OK to meet today?

I received a second message, which started to make me think I must have been quite keen to meet, as I've never before arranged to meet the next day. However, I always believed an offer was best taken once there, rather than think it will return. Even more so now, seeing as I had no job to slave for, no girlfriend to share a peach with.

[Text message]
To: London's Calling
Yes same time and place?

I sat up and stared at my phone screen like I had just matched all five numbers on the lottery and was only awaiting the bonus ball. Hoping a message would contain a little more detail or at least a reference to a conversation I could use, a clue to help see their face or a feature, anything to not have to go into it completely blind.

[Text message]
From: London's Calling
Yeah.

Blind it was.

[Text message]
To: London's Calling
Great, see you soon.

I arrived early and waited outside, in front of the cafe. Having no clue as to whom I was looking out for forced me to offer weird stares and crooked smiles to anyone that passed. After catching a reflection of myself in the window, I decided the best thing to do was go inside before I got arrested for being a creep. I entered a clustered shop. Despite the bell over the door, it was very quiet, but not a soothing quiet, more like a calm before the storm quiet, unsettling to me anyway. Four people were present. One elderly couple sitting opposite one another, both hiding behind a newspaper. They say conversation is important in a relationship. Attractive personalities as opposed to a personality that relies on just being attractive, which seems to be the case these days. I guess not much has changed, apart from the newspapers becoming phones. Although it seemed more plausible that the elderly couple would have run out of things to talk about. Unless they had always been like that, who knew. I continued to look around; it was not your usual branded shop. I assumed quirky was the idea, but I found it a little strange. Four or five manikins had been axed and divided within the décor. Legs that were lamps, arms that were, well, arms of the chairs. The heads had been sliced open at the top and placed on most tables, housing sugar sachets and stirrers. There were also two heads hanging by a chain on a door toward the back. A bearded male and a dolled up female indicating a single, shared toilet. An owner who obviously wanted to be unique, or make a statement of some kind, or maybe had just put too much thought into the theme. No theme became the theme, or maybe an abnormal method to warn off squatters. That would definitely have worked, I felt. I approached the counter and ordered a breakfast tea. I was instructed to take a seat by the punk rocker dressed barista where I then took that moment to update my mystery human and send a message I couldn't ever imagine sending again in my life.

[Text message]
To: London's Calling
I'm sitting in the far corner in front of the blue leg lamp on a table that has the head wearing sunglasses and green lipstick.

I wasn't even sure if the person I was meeting was male or female. To be honest, I wasn't bothered, as I was more curious as to the why than the who. My tea arrived in a normal white mug, which I looked at as if I'd never seen one before. The infectious ambience had transformed me; and I had become unfamiliar with normality and living on the other side of the spectrum where I was more used to drinking tea from a hand. As I took a sip from my ghastly mug, I looked up and noticed someone approaching the door. A tall slim man in his middle thirties entered, carrying a cycling helmet, his bright yellow t-shirt with a tiger face catching my eye and triggering something. I had seen it before, and it did make sense he could be wearing the same clothes. I surely was, another benefit from my lucky creaseless shirt. He noticed me straight away and walked over with a huge smile on his face. He had a well-groomed beard praised by a fruity and overwhelming amount of aftershave. I stood to greet him and we shook hands, whilst I held a confused frown on my face. He must have understood because he quickly jumped in.

"George!"

"George. I had you saved as London's Calling."

"Yes, London's Calling, that was funny when you said that."

I didn't remember saying it or why I even did say it. I still had no clue what it meant. George placed his cycling helmet on the manikin head and said:

"Safety first!" whilst pointing at the helmet and me. "Hahahaha."

His laugh was familiar. As he continued with his uncanny chuckle, I observed his movements and mannerisms like a hawk, my brain going wild with flashbacks but still not placing him, or why we had arranged to meet.

"Would you like anything else?" Pointing at my tea.

"I'm good thank you."

George walked over to the counter and ordered an espresso off the young barista before returning and sitting opposite me. A moment of silence occurred amid a couple of smirks and head bops.

"So how are you feeling?" he asked, holding a sympathetic look on his face.

"A little rough around the edges, but I'm used to it."

"You didn't seem too sure about what to do with…" He started clicking his fingers. "Gabby?" he eventually trickled out.

"Oh. I'm sure it will be ok it's just…"

The barista brought over George's espresso and placed it in front of him.

"…Women," George spilled out, interrupting me.

I caught a soft-top tucked lip look from the barista as she walked away. George then removed a stirrer from the manikin head and began stirring his espresso, followed by a loud sip before placing it back down.

"I was in the same boat my friend. The main thing to remember is babies."

"Babies?"

"Babies."

"What babies?"

"Just babies. Tiny humans, that shit and cry all night and suck your lady's firm breasts down to the floor whilst sucking energy and life from us. Babies."

"Oh." I looked around to see if anyone was listening.

"And money. It doesn't matter how you are in the sheets. Pounds are chosen over pounding, as the money, the money is the security for the babies and then we just become a stranger."

George took another sip from his espresso whilst keeping eye contact with me before I felt able to respond.

"My problem is not babies or money, it's me."

"Yes, like it was for me, you are the problem. But that's your problem, not to be worked at as a couple? For better or for worse, right? My old girlfriend always said it would be different after I proposed. She would only help and support me after I spend thousands on a diamond ring? What is it, a magic fucking ring? Hahahaha."

George's laugh began to attack the room.

"I don't think Gabby cares too much about marriage."

"They all say this my friend. Let me tell you she does."

"You don't know her."

"I don't need to know her. It shows from you."

I wasn't quite sure what to say so I didn't say anything. I wasn't even sure what was happening; it felt like some kind of un-arranged therapy session mixed with some kind of sales pitch.

"Freedom," he continued. "Enjoy. I can give you an opportunity to have money and a stress-free life. Not constant control on what you should be doing bla bla bla. This is why I came to London, my friend, to get away from the rabbit shit. Here I could start again. Why choose one wife and many problems when you can choose unlimited girlfriends and zero problems? Hahahaha."

George's chuckle again attacked the room. He banged on the table a couple of times, making the elderly couple peek out from behind their newspapers. I was obliged to give them the same soft top, tucked lip the young barista gave me moments before, hoping the ground would swallow me whole and I'd disappear. George's phone then began ringing, an out-dated high-pitched English national anthem, at which he moved his shoulders up and down whilst smiling at me for the moment before he answered.

"Hello."

His tone became soft and he held a professional and clearer articulation.

"Ok sure. Yes, I have the perfect guy."

He smiled and winked at me.

"I will send you a message with what is needed from you and get that all arranged…"

"OK bye."

He hung up and put the phone down on the table.

"You're free tonight, right?"

"For what?"

"Your first client! London's Calling baby, hahahaha."

And then it hit me. It seemed more reasonable that something like this would be harder to forget than remember. When we met the night before he was with three girls I noticed dancing in the corner of the room, during my drop phase. As I approached them, he stopped me dead in my tracks, like a security guard protecting a celebrity. He began explaining that he was with them, and furthermore they were "colleagues" of a "company" he managed, the kind of "company" that offered "company". Mumbling in my ear for shit knows how long. I was just observing the ladies and would zone in and out with him. Basically just nodding along, laughing when he did, which explained why I was more familiar with his chuckle than his face. I'd barely looked at him.

Toward the end of our drunken meet, he asked if it were something I would consider doing, as the "company" were currently looking to expand. Women were also seeking "company" from his "company". My being in a drunken, penniless state at the time, I jumped at it. It took us a while to exchange numbers due to the states we were both in. During that I remember him continuing to say how businesswomen who visit the city don't have time for a relationship, ringing him up all hours of the day and night. That's when I said it: London's Calling. We both laughed for a strong two minutes. I don't know why we laughed. I can't even say it was a 'you had to be there' moment because it was simply only because of that. I guess it was a moment you had to be *us* moment. A moment of a quick-witted remark which translated wrongly, where I meant something else. We both just understood. The drunken crawler's language working its top form.

"You remember the three girls I was with last night?"

"Vaguely."

"I've just taken them on. I'm in charge of making sure everyone is sociable before reporting back to the boss.

Well sociable and flexible if you know what I mean. Not that the girls need to pass a test or anything, but I kind of hint to them that it can help them get the job."

"So you slept with them?"

"Of course. All three. At the same time."

"Does that not make you feel guilty?"

"Guilty? No. Well I do feel slightly guilty after persuading one of the girls to go in the back door knowing she was taking a horse riding lessons today, hahahaha."

I sat holding a fake smile for a moment whilst looking out at the elderly couple wishing I also had a newspaper to hide behind. I was also intrigued, and felt a distraction would be good. Even better, a chance to earn money to give Gabby, so I felt to enquire further into the madness.

"So how does it work?"

"I will usually message you with inquiries. If you are free, the where, the time and the who will follow."

"And the attire?"

"Attire? Sorry, I don't know this word."

"Clothes."

"Oh. Shirt, trousers something presentable. But nothing that stands out too much as you want to blend in, keeping it discreet. And always remember protection. Safety first," he said whilst pointing at the helmet on the manikin head again.

"I assume you take a commission?"

"You assume correct. The commission is thirty per cent. I will arrange to meet you once a week to collect it from you. So how does it sound? Are you up for it?"

"Maybe."

"Maybe come on! Look, go home relax a bit. Get ready for tonight, try it, and if you don't like it you can leave. I'll even let you keep the commission."

"Ok."

George stood and picked up his helmet and chuckled a little more about that before putting out his hand. I stood to shake it.

"Oh, and an alias name too, anything you can think of?"

"Nothing right now, can I let you know later?"

"Of course. Speak soon, goodbye."

"Bye."

George left the shop calm and collected, like an on-duty small town sheriff leaving a bar midday. Probably chuckling more about the back door girl as he jumped up onto his horse and rode off into the sunset.

It seemed sensible at the time to go visit the one person who would have no reason to lie to me, even if she always seemed to lie to herself. The very woman who told me to always do what makes me happy; to just get on with it and never look back. She was someone capable of sugar coating a war. Sometimes this was needed, a different perspective, no matter if one agrees or not. It certainly helped open my mind, and open minded is something I needed to be.

I stood outside a house that looked more uninviting than Buckingham palace, the guards replaced by large garden hedges either side of the door where a camera gawked at you, where I would always cover before knocking.

"Who is it?" a worried voice called out from behind the door.

"It's me," I replied with a known yet more worried voice.

The door opened and I was warmly greeted with a hug and kiss. We made our way to our usual heart to heart area in the kitchen and I perched on my usual stool amongst the breakfast worktop whilst the smell of bleach and cleaning perfume surrounded us.

"Would you like a tea?" She asked

"Anything stronger?"

"Coffee?"

"Very funny."

"Darling, you know we don't keep any alcohol in this house. Leonardo has been sober for ten years now."

Ah yes, Leonardo. The smooth talking, sharply dressed, poetic, sight for sore eyes man who always wore shorts no matter the weather, the kind of shorts that were more testicle than material. They met on a photo-shoot, Leo being the photographer during the days my mother aspired to act and model. He also worked on other kinds of sets, the erotic kind. I guess the divorce between my parents seems obvious once that comes out, but when comparing the two men in her life it isn't exactly difficult to place any blame. Leonardo told my mother her eyes belonged to those of an angel in heaven and her presence more warming than hell. (When I said he was poetic, I meant he tried to be). An award-winning restaurant and penthouse hotel suite followed that statement, and the knickers were immediately off. Whereas my dad approached her in a local pub and offered her some paracetamol because he thought her eyes looked puffy, followed by a sloppy burger from a burger van, a visit to his messy flat, and the knickers were off, a few hours later.

"Charlie!" the name was announced as Leo's balls entered the kitchen before he did.

Charlie isn't my name. He called me Charlie as he referred to me as Charles Dickens because at the time we met I was very deep in ink. Like I said, he tried.

"Hello Fagin," I replied, standing to shake his hand.

"Fagin? What is this Fagin?"

A classic example of the man's intelligence, he referred to me as Charles Dickens but was unfamiliar with his work and what he was saying.

"Nothing he's just being silly," my mother jumped in.

"So are you still writing?" Fagin asked.

"Nothing that would be of use to you."

"Don't be going on about that please," my mother jumped in again.

"What did I say?" I questioned sarcastically.

I had caught Leo going through a note pad of mine when I stayed with my mother one summer. After a while, I returned the favour by watching a blue film he had worked on, only to find the narrative was very similar to one of my nearly finished short stories, one a lot of blood, sweat and beers had gone into. It was tainted with Leo's vision, and my mothers acting role, nothing explicit but the whole thing had been laughable.

"I know what you meant." my mother continued.

"What? The plot of a serial killer posing as a police informant is the plot of most porn films; it's an easy mistake."

Fagin's film *Serial Driller* never got released in the end. Production cut his costs and refused to release it. He didn't quite think it through, I mean why would people not enjoy the idea of mixing sex with murders along with my mothers acting? He thought it was a sure success. The reason it bothered me was because it was the only story I came even close to finishing, and he had tainted it with his childish adaptation. So that was one story I had to forget, continuing my path of unfinished material.

"Chess, easy mistake," the stallion replied.

I faced my mother with folded lips. He always said 'chess' instead of yes which was amusing at the time I met him, but after a few years it became the most ear abusing word. I could never handle hearing it without folding up.

"Darling, we're just going to have a chat."

"Chess, Ok."

"Check mate," I interrupted.

"Pardon?"

"Nothing, he's winding you up, just give us a minute."

"I will go take the bath."

"Where are you taking it?"

"Stop!" My mother's patience wearing thin.

Leo and his shorts left the room to go take the bath somewhere and I was finally alone with my mother.

"So what's new?" She began

"I was offered a job."

"I thought you already had a job."

"I left."

"Because of this new job?"

"No."

"Oh. How is Gabby? Any grandkids on the way?"

"What? No, She kicked me out."

"Why?"

"Mum please, just listen."

"You just said…"

"Yes, I know." Interrupting her.

"Darling, the main thing you need to remember is, for a relationship to work, you need to communicate," interrupting me this time.

"Oh fuck."

By which she meant: she did all the communication, and Fagin did as he was told. From which I understood that it may be easier, at times, or as time went on, to surrender. But I just had too much stubbornness, which I saw as drive, the drive to do it my own way.

"So what's this new job?"

"Gigolo."

"Oh. Well, what ever makes you happy."

"Really?"

"What do you want me to say?"

"Something else, anything else."

"It doesn't matter what I say, you never listen."

"I'm in a difficult position and need to earn money."

"Well, if you're doing it just to earn money, then its not going to work out."

"Why not?"

"Because you'll always need money, but you'll also always leave when it's something you don't enjoy, and then you will just be in the exact same position as before."

"Maybe."

"Well you know who would be best to talk to about this."

"No chance," interrupting her

"He's been around this more than I have, he even used to entertain people himself so would have more knowledge on everything."

"I'd rather eat a horse's ass than talk to him."

"Well, he can advice you on eating ass too."

"Please stop."

"Sorry, I was just joking around. Look it doesn't matter what you do, its how you do it. You can clean toilets or be a lawyer, the difference is how they look after themselves. Eat well, work out, have a healthy body and mind and the title or what you do for money doesn't matter. It's who you are as a person, the job doesn't make you the person."

"Ok, I need to go."

"This was a short visit. You sure you don't want a tea?"

"No thank you."

"Or some food? I can make you something."

"No, I need to go."

"Do you need to stay here?"

"No, I'm going to stay at Madhav's old place."

"Oh, Madhav. How is he? Still working hard at his parent's place?"

"Yes"

"Such a good kid that one"

"Ok, bye."

"I'll tell Leo you said bye."

"Why?"

"Because it's polite."

"That's what I'm trying to avoid."

"Stop, come here."

I stood up, hugged my mother and swiftly left to think things through. To plan my next chess move.

[6]

On the train journey back, I sat in an empty carriage with a full mind. I wasn't used to the missing people as I had experienced only cramped carriages before, the nose to armpit status. That time felt more like a proper ride. The wobbling moved me more. The announcements were clearly heard instead of straining my ears trying to figure out where I was, hoping each stop was mine. A rush of thoughts matching the speed of the train through a darkened tunnel, nothing clear, just like the view through the windows. The only option was the many overwhelming crashes. A rhythm of thuds flooded a tunnel vision and began sparking my emotions. Heavy thumps of worry harmonising with a high-pitched squealing of joy, triggering an overload of anxiousness. The shuddering and high-pitched sounds soon stopped, but the thoughts only started. Overthinking was an understatement for what I was experiencing. A thousand scenarios ran at once on what could possibly happen if I took on the up and coming role.

The thing with anxious thinking is the ability to reassure oneself. To turn off the road of concern and take the exit onto the calm freeway. I have done it many a time. The way is to focus more on how I feel before any further thought occurs, as opposed to allowing the thinking to affect how I feel. Then I'm always grateful for the things I have in my life, the things that make, and have made, me happy. Fear is imaginary, whereas memories were reality. And yes, you can't predict the future but you certainly can control how you go into it. Once I am relaxed and clear-headed and back trusting how I felt about it all, I begin to think things through in smaller steps, breaking down the concerns and erasing any further negative thoughts. A good old divide and conquer approach, but with good intentions.

The train began to slow for the next stop, which should have been my stop. My focus was on the person standing on the platform as the train came to a halt. A pregnant woman boarded, and despite it being an empty carriage I stood up to offer my seat. It was the closest to her, so she took it and thanked me with a smile. I sat back down beside her. The train continued on its way when I noticed the station sign, which forced a loud tut from my mouth, catching the attention of the woman. We shared a concerned look, which prompted the need to explain.

"That was my stop."

She smirked and began rattling around in her handbag, pulling out her phone. I couldn't help but spy. A list of baby names separated in two categories had caught my eye and I immediately thought about Gabby and our baby. A slap from reality which hit hard, especially when the woman beside me seemed a lot more mature and comfortable in her life about raising a child, despite riding the tube. I wasn't quite ready to think about that, so once again turned off the road of concern, putting my thoughts onto the freeway. I thought about the name I would use for the job, starting to get excited about it, even feeling like a secret agent, a new identity where I could create a new life, have some fun on top of the other fun. The train approached the next stop so I quickly scanned the pregnant woman's baby names, taking one from the boy's list and one from the girls. I waited close to the doors ready to exit, feeling excited. I'm not sure why but I had a warm feeling inside, maybe it was the idea of having no one to answer to. Who knew, but it felt nice. My eye then caught an outplaced sticker on the glass of the door. An abstract drawing of a bird mixed with an evolutional human structure and robotic features, a short verse besides it.

I used to stand proud and walk
And now I fly.
I used to be feared
And now I cry.
I used to eat what and when I pleased,
And now everything just tastes like cheese.
I used to have companions at just a glance,
And now I have to bloody dance, for just a chance,
And with no arms just looks bizarre, watching my back
for cats and cars,
Evolution gone too far!
So what's the point of being me?
Well, I may be a pigeon but at least I'm free.

- Someone. Once

I felt somewhat inspired, a feeling I hadn't had for a while. Although it was hidden away, it was nice to know the writer in me was still alive. I also took the words to heart and more so as a sign, to stay focused on the good instead of allowing the bad to ruin my focus. I stepped off the train and started to repeat my new name over and over so it was embedded within me. After a few rehearsals, it stuck, and grew on me, more and more. Benjamin Joy. Coincidental or written in the stars, who knew. It didn't matter, as I felt the initials were very suiting to the position, and with my alias carved in stone I would go on to prepare the rest of my starter kit. And, I had just the guy to help me.

[Text Message]
To: MainManMads
Are you at your shop?

[Text Message]
From: MainManMads
Of course.

[Text Message]
To: MainManMads
Pint?

[Text Message]
From: MainManMads
Of course.

[Text message]
To: MainManMads
Meet you at the dungeon in twenty minutes?

[Text message]
From: MainManMads
Ok.

Madhav's family owned a pharmacy which he took over a few years back. He was the one who introduced me to 'snoozers' which I got for back door prices; it's how we started a friendship, really. We met at a summer youth club when we were thirteen. A familiar environment yet an unfamiliar situation. It was a time teens began sexually experimenting, most teenagers anyway. I would often sneak my summer love into the caretaker's room. The caretaker was never there of course; it would always be at lunchtime when he did his rounds of the building, taking a good hour in doing so due to a gammy leg. The room was quite large but felt small due to stacked junk from everything and anything he had collected during his routes over the years. It also contained an aroma I would usually only smell in a curry house on the odd Saturday night treat with the family. It wasn't romantic but we were teens, the interest in expensive taste and glamorised surroundings were yet to be programmed. All we cared about was privacy. So I would go there most days with my girlfriend. Madhav had witnessed the encounters several times before I had witnessed him. It seemed I wasn't the only one who had noticed the caretakers schedule to seize a window of opportunity. He would hide away in a corner so he could eat his lunch in peace without the rest of the teens questioning his mum's food. Madhav was Indian if you hadn't guessed already. So you can imagine the uproar when the teens, only used to turkey dinosaurs and smiley potato faces, saw Madhav's vegetable curry. They'd say things like: "how's your diarrhoea today?" I never said anything, I like Indian food. It was my third visit with my summer love before Madhav had given away his hiding spot. I was around the knee area when a load of broken chairs started to fall, knocking over several more things, a waterfall of furniture. This pushed my girlfriend to pure worry and she bailed out the room before the junk had even settled. Once everything had stopped, Madhav became visible. A little greasy haired ball of innocence perched on a milk crate, eating out of a plastic container, a stained yellow one. Holding a fork in his hand and a concerned look on his face. Madhav's presence had explained the tumble and his stained pot had explained the spiced fragrance the room captured. We spoke often of that scenario throughout the holidays and built a relationship based on exchange; him getting hold of certain items such as painkillers, were worth more than gold where I lived, and I'd help him build his confidence with the girls. Madhav was good looking with a chiselled jawline. Many took to his exotic features. He was sweet

67

like honey although his approach was similar to that of a bee. I merely helped him adjust, to be the prize and not so much a disturbed hive. Loyalty and trust soon followed our interests, and we soon had a friendship. He wasn't the usual suspect but he had a big heart and I liked that. There were maybe millions just like him but none where I was from.

Once I reached our local, I ordered two pints of beer and sat toward the back tucked away from any wondering ears. Not that there were many, it was hardly busy and was more the kind of place that homed homeless-looking men who only had the microwave to go back and talk to. It was small and dark, somewhere we'd been going to for over a decade. It even had the same paint, just more marks, war scars of the many karaoke and religious celebrations that fought there. A hidden cornered room, a pool table where spilt drinks stained the cloth. Shaky wooden legs from carrying the many drunken secrets. It was a dungeon, but it was our dungeon.

It wasn't long before Madhav came crashing through the doors with the usual concerned look on his face. It soon changed to a huge smile after noticing myself or more than likely the beer I had waiting for him. He then stopped off by the bar before coming over, ordering two more beers, which was a typical tell that he couldn't stay long. He held one pint up to me at the bar and I held mine up from where I sat and we both began drinking, finishing them off simultaneously. He then picked up the other, came over, sat opposite me and said:

"What doesn't kill you?"

"Gets you drunker."

We clinked glasses and both took a gulp.

"I can't stay long, I have a new girl watching the shop."

"Do you remember Diamond?"

"The hooker? Of course, she was gorgeous. I still can't believe you felt you needed to pay, we could have just gone to a bar."

"We did. It was the same night. And you hooked up with that tall German girl and I hooked up with her friend."

"Oh yes," he said whilst gazing upwards.

"I didn't feel I needed to pay anyway, I wanted to."

"Why, is she here?" He began eagerly looking around the dungeon.

"No, she's not. Why would she be here?"

"I don't know, why mention her then?"

"I just wanted to know how you felt about it."

"I don't know. Perception really."

"What do you mean?"

"Well, if you think about it, most men start by spending time and money on women in hope of getting the same result, right? This often isn't even the case, so the reality is, most men are left having spent more money and more time and don't even get the ass."

"Yeah."

"Do you remember that guy that worked for me, shit, I forget his name, the weird one, always stared at the wall?"

I shook my head.

"Anyway, he came in one day all happy about some date where he spent two hundred pounds on dinner and she left when they got outside the restaurant."

"Oh yes, I do remember him. Glasses?"

"Yeah. He said it was because she just got a new kitten and needed to go home and feed it. I said she basically said when she's around you she'd rather go home and feed her own pussy."

"Hahahaha."

We both filled the dungeon with laughter before Madhav continued.

"He didn't know what to say mate, his tongue was flapping around like he was performing cunnilingus on a ghost."

We continued laughing and then sat catching our breath for a moment.

"Ok, so what do you think about it from her perspective?" I gave a suggestive look.

"Who, Diamond?"

"Yeah."

"Like if I were her?"

"Yeah."

"It's my dream job."

"What?"

"No strings attached and getting paid."

"I need some bits from the shop." I gave another suggestive look.

"Wait. Really?"

"Yeah."

"Does Gabby know?"

"We broke up."

"Oh, ok, good."

"Good?"

"Not good as in that's good, just good…"

"I'm kidding. I knew what you meant."

"Can you get me in?" he said with an even bigger grin on his face.

"In where?"

"The job!"

"I haven't even started, so I'm not going to ask if I can recruit."

"Yeah true. Give it a couple of days and then ask."

"Can you get me some bits or not?"

"Protection?"

"Yeah."

"Be good to have lubricant too. Ooh, and I have just got the latest proscribed blue pills, came in last week, I call them fuck buddies. They are so strong, someone our age would get an erection for a day just by smelling them."

"Great sales pitch. Whatever you can get, how much do you want?"

"Get me like fifty pounds."

"Ok. I need to ask another favour."

"Ok?"

"Can I stay in the shop flat, just until I pick myself up?"

"Of course. Where are you staying now?"

"A hotel."

"Yeah, it's fine."

"Thanks."

"Ok, I got to go. I'll meet you around the back in ten minutes?"

"Ok, I need to withdraw some cash."

"Do you need any snoozers?"

"Maybe."

"Ok, I will give you some just in case."

We both finished our drinks in one and left in two, in such excitement, although I think Madhav was more excited than I was. He skipped back to his shop and I went to withdraw some cash before heading to meet him. Our usual back door spot neighboured a hidden alleyway, perfect for our meet and sweep. I apprehensively waited close to the unalarmed fire door longer than expected, but I reminded myself that Madhav was a man of his word, especially when it involved some quick cash. As he crashed through the door several minutes later, my initial thought as to why he was taking so long was brushed over. Different supplies, of course. In fact, I should have wondered how come he was so quick. He handed me a bulging plastic bag containing enough condoms to last a group of eager graduates four seasons on spring break, a load of lubricant tubes that could fill a bathtub and boxes upon boxes of 'fuck buddies'. What was even more surprising was what he said next.

"Is that enough?"

"Yes Mads."

"Ok. Here's the key for the flat."

"Thanks. I need to go grab my things."

"And there are a couple boxes of snoozers in there somewhere if you need them."

"Ok thanks."

"Let me know if you need anything."

"Will do."

"Oh, and remember to break up the fuck buddies and only take half, otherwise you'll be pissing in your face for a day."

I handed him the money and walked away, gripping the bag that made me feel like I had just carried out my own lone loot, and in fear that if caught I would demote those labelled with nymphomania down to just horny. I rushed back to the hotel to collect my belongings, stopping off at a nearby off licence for some much needed alcoholic beverages. Once I reached the flat, I dropped my stuff onto the sofa and gratefully exhaled all my contained air before collapsing next to the bags. Opening a cold can, I looked around an interior of fast food packaging, old clothes and boxes of out-dated medicines. Even the boiler was out-dated and would randomly fire up during the night, so it was just left off. I guess the cold walls suited the abode, but it became home, well, a home away from home anyway.

A few cans in, I began thinking about Gabby. Before I met her I was never actually one for relationships. What I mean is, I felt I always had the heart and thoughtful traits that suited being with someone, but there was always a time, a pattern if you will, where I could only maintain those traits for a certain period before I became uninterested and started to rethink the meaning and purpose of it all. Maybe formed from constantly messing up or being made to feel like I had anyway, who knew. I always wondered if the women prior to Gabby actually knew how to switch that on and off, or were even aware that they were doing it. Or was it just something that was built in, an unconscious uncontrollable superpower, as such, where brain shatters brawn, taking the man from me and simply making more use of it by putting it in manipulation?

I never accused my pasts any less than myself. I was well aware that having a laid-back, spectating persona escorted with forgetful characteristics invited confrontation every now and again. Walking away from it only seemed to make it worse. And I certainly wouldn't take the male corner on it and state that women are to blame, as I endorse the same thing where women are the ones being controlled by certain alpha mannerisms, where brawn took charge. I call those the Rumpelstiltskin relations. Where someone with good intentions, along with an ambitious mind-set and self-knowing capabilities, or merely an overall love for life itself, battles with the other who just has the need for constant blame and complain; the "that's life" attitude. So one is focused and working hard in spinning that straw into gold, whilst their partner stands behind them spinning that gold back into straw.

I then began to have doubts about human relations completely, which may have formed after my meeting with George. It did make sense, suiting human nature to portion and spend time with many, as opposed to the monogamous stories we are trained and forced to believe in and suffer, not share, with someone. A combination of fantasy and animalistic instincts simply creating nothing but a concoction of poison that we sip on, watching life wasting away as we stubbornly force a dream. The evidence pointed more towards me just not caring enough, but with Gabby I did, and I began to see that I was to blame. I also couldn't seem to work out what it was I needed to do, and what was more worrying is I didn't even know if I would get a chance to try.

[Text message]
From: London's Calling
Ready for tonight?

[Text message]
To: London's Calling
Let's do it.

[Text message]
From: London's Calling
11:00 PM
****** Hotel

[Text message]
To: London's Calling
Great.

[Text message]
From: London's Calling
Have you thought of an alias name?

[Text message]
To: London's Calling
Yes. Benjamin Joy.

[Text message]
From: London's Calling
Big Ben I like it. When you arrive wait in the lobby and let me know when you are there.

[Text message]
To: London's Calling
Sure.

[7]

The hotel atmosphere took me back like a gust of wind. Surroundings that could withhold the roar of a coliseum but only presented a graceful ambience that injected tranquillity. I admired a huge room that was filled with people, but it still felt empty. A massive, unique lighting display gleamed like the sun when you looked at it, but showered down only a soft moonlight, highlighting the shimmering marble floor and brick walls. Superior trickery that captured the brilliance of an exterior design hitched with the smothering of interior warmness.

I began walking towards a large circled sofa that sat in the centre of the room like a merry go round, my shoes echoing from the marble floor with each step. I sat down and observed the people present. Well-mannered conversations flowed as well as the air that came from their whispers. Everyone seemed important. Not to a family member or friend, but to a business or organisation of some kind. I took my phone out from my pocket and sent in my arrival before continuing to listen to the body language around me. It wasn't long before I heard a voice hissing out "Benjamin," a ninja-like approach from a man with silver hair. He stood in front of me in a three-piece grey suit accompanied by the unknown but striking scent of an exotic flower. I stood and shook his hand before following behind like a lost puppy. I was unsure who the guy was, maybe an assistant of some kind or a manager to someone who would need to take extra precautions. Although it seemed highly unlikely I would run into Madonna, I did however begin to question what I had I got myself into.

We took the lift to the 4th floor where we continued walking down a narrow corridor, so long that the end was a blur, even to those with twenty-twenty vision. The floor was layered with a soft maroon carpet my shoes sank into each step. The style was completely different from the lobby. It still held class but it was more like an old country house with antique dressing, all delicately lit by wall lamps that made the corridor even narrower, forcing a shoulder to shoulder stroll into single file. I followed behind like a puppy amongst a dimmed silence.

"Sit down," he firmly proclaimed.

Hearing the silver-haired ninja suddenly speak through cushioned silence, caused my heart to skip a beat. We sat beside one another on a small wooden bench with a leather top placed halfway down the corridor, a rest point maybe for those who couldn't make it to the end in one go. We faced each other on a small comfortable bench. The exotic scent, overpowered by the alcohol on his breath, struck me as he spoke.

"So, she really wants to dance for you. So just make sure you don't avoid that. Sit back and enjoy it and then you can pretty much do... have you got protection?"

"Of course."

"Fine, good. Yes, so my only rule is you stay protected. Anything goes so do as you please. The main focus is on pleasing her of course."

"Of course," I said with a subtle smirk.

"We've been married twenty years, she has a high drive, and she's lovely you'll have a good time."

I couldn't quite believe what I was hearing. It all seemed dream-like but the reality was, I was sat nose touching opposite a man, or more specifically a husband who held a smile on his face as he ran through an encounter with his wife. As for me, I had to sit there pretending I was used to it. He then pointed further down the corridor where my head naturally followed the aim of his finger.

"Room 502, have fun."

Turning back towards him, naturally expecting more alcohol fumes whilst I held a hesitant thank you on my tongue, I found he was halfway down the first half of the corridor, bolting back towards the elevator like a prisoner on death row that had just noticed the main entrance left open. I looked down toward the room, then back again toward the lift, into which he had disappeared. I took a second to reflect before standing and making my move toward the room.

It was my turn to feel on death row, on judgement day, passing the other rooms and watching the numbers counting down to my execution. The exotic alcohol was removed from the air and all I could smell was wood and leather from the antiques. The carpet no longer felt soft either, just worn in and greasy, and with each step I felt like I had to restrain myself from slipping. Two of the wall lamps were flickering, which took my focus away from the room numbers until I was up close to the lights. As soon as I reached them, they shut off completely. I looked over to the door where a darkened 502 could be made out. With one last glance down the corridor, I lifted my arm and gave the usual Morse code knock you seem to do with a bent index finger when someone's expecting you. Then I stepped backwards, further into the shadows of the broken lamps. Half my body was facing the door, the other half was facing the direction of the elevator, ready to bail and join the husband in messing up the hotel's carpet.

All my senses were heightened. Slow breaths left my nose as my chest raised up and down. My eyes were focused and ready to analyse everything and anything that appeared. I began to hear movement, a rattling behind the door followed by the sound of high heels clicking against the wooden floor, my ears on form just like my eyes. Helping my brain to relate that feminine sound and provide the reassurance I needed. Suddenly and unexpectedly the handle moved down quicker than a western draw and the door slung open quicker than a bullet would leave a cowboy's gun. My eyes blurred like I had been shot. All I could see was the outline of my killer standing in front of me. It felt like an hour before my eyes went back to their usual short-sighted opinion, but I was relieved they did, so shocked to see what stood in front of me. Dark smooth skin with thick marble magnetic green eyes I could feel pulling me closer. One side of her hair was long, and the other was cut short with a kind of kink to it which bounced with each head movement. She had big lips with a small but noticeable scar crossing the top, only making her more endearing, like an enemy of James Bond. She didn't need a "my eyes are up here T-shirt", she needed a "my breasts are down there" hat, as all I did was admire her face. My body fully facing hers as I waited cautiously for the invite, as I couldn't picture them together. She was certainly a woman who would wear the trousers. He did have trousers on but I wouldn't be surprised if she made him wear a thong underneath.

"Come in come in," she said with a soft lisp.

She stepped aside and walked further into the room. I closed the door behind me, leaving all thoughts of the husband in the corridor. I felt safe so I no longer cared, and didn't care to add my nose to the list of sticking things in. Once I was in the room I could feel the vast size of it. It wasn't your standard sixty-pound a night, the sort of place you took someone during the exploring stage, when you didn't care to impress. It was classy, very classy and suited the kind of get together. The whole room was lit with candles, the first set placed along the floor like a mini runway leading to another room. The others were placed around a fancy bath and highlighted the shiny copper piping and Rose petals that were scattered around the edging. A romantic set-up but something that didn't suit that kind of get together. The thought of having to share a bath with a stranger didn't exactly put me at ease and all I wanted was the support of my "fuck buddy". She reached for my hand and led me down the candlelit runway into a large bedroom where a king-size bed dominated the space.

"I'm drinking champagne. What would you like?"

Many expensive bottles were displayed on a large wooden unit smiling up at me.

"Champagne is fine, thank you."

When she picked up the champagne bottle it revealed the hiding place to a small silver metal plate containing a few lines of white powder. She noticed me noticing, so I quickly acted to avoid any awkwardness of declining.

"Can I use the toilet?"

"Sure, it's over there."

I entered the bathroom, locked the door and stood standing facing a large mirror for a second before I removed a "fuck buddy" from my wallet, using the sink tap water to wash it down. As I came up I saw Madhav in the mirror, a vague but clear enough image of him reminding me to break up the pill and only take half the amount. It was too late. Worried my whole body would turn into an ironing board, I flushed the toilet and made my way back to the bedroom to finish my drink in one go, in the hope it would keep the rest of my limbs loose.

"Thirsty. Would you like another?"

"Sure, thank you."

As she began pouring me another drink I noticed the lines of powder had been visited but not because I spotted any attack from the plate. She had stashed a little bit in one of her nostrils, and despite the put off she was still something to appreciate.

"Did you meet my husband?"

"I did."

"What did you think of him?"

"He smelt nice."

She displayed a radiant smile which made her scar blend into her lip and became unnoticeable.

"He's watching the golf down at the bar. There's some big event on, I don't really know. Do you like golf?"

"Not particularly."

"Good, it's an old man's sport. He gets more excited about that than me these days. I always say a sport matches the stamina of a man."

"That's certainly one way of looking at it."

"What's another?"

"Maybe there just comes a point where taking your time and playing smart, as opposed to quick, is more suiting."

"I prefer my way."

"Then so do I."

Our eyes shared a smile and our lips shared a stare before she continued to interrogate.

"Do you have good stamina?"

"I do, I think."

"You should use it as much as you can. Certain things don't work as well when you get older, if you know what I mean."

"I do."

"How old are you?"

"Old enough to get it up and young enough to keep it up."

"Very clever. Lovely to meet you Benjamin."

"You too, cheers."

We clinked glasses and continued to stare into one another's eyes as we sipped the champagne. I was looking through green windows to her mind, where the many thoughts could be seen. I decided to act quickly.

"I heard you wanted to dance for me?"

"Would you like that?"

"Maybe."

She smiled and reached for my hand and led me to the sofa beside the bed. Once I was sat down she walked over to a portable speaker and played some soft instrumental music and began dancing slowly, in front of me, just out of reach. After a few distant twists and turns, she came close and moved down onto her knees and began stroking my thighs whilst looking into my eyes. Sudden rushes of warmth began to run through my body and a blue tint covered my vision. My focus was all on her and the rest of the room disappeared. A rush of blood bounced from my feet, all the way up to my face where it stayed, an overwhelming blushing feel. My heart was beating fast; each beat provided a strong thump against my chest in sync with the music. The fuck buddy, along with her stare which was just as powerful as Medusa's, rapidly turned a certain part of me to stone.

Noticing my excitement, she made her way over to the bed and laid down, keeping her eyes on mine as I began to scan further south. My eyes ran up her legs where I soon noticed she wasn't wearing any underwear. Her legs began parting slowly and I penetratingly stared until her legs were fully stretched, revealing an area that was smooth and neat. It was very appealing, like untouched snow or an artist's vision of this region belonging to the Virgin Mary. I stood up and took to it quicker than a Christian who had just seen the gates of heaven opening. I didn't get to spend much time there, nor did I get to speak to the all-mighty. I was rejected. She pulled me up and kissed me hard, cushioned by her lips.

I removed my clothes before removing the raincoat from its packaging as she slipped off her dress. We shared a moment of innocence before I moved slowly towards her and kissed her neck. She laid back as I attended to her head, easing it gently to the pillow. We were like young lovers. I gripped her hands and stretched her arms over her head. We continued to exchange kisses as our bodies came together and fitted perfectly with every slow movement.

"Wait!" she said unexpectedly.

And the prom night was over. She reached to the bedside table and removed a large, mechanical, pink rubber cock from the top drawer.

"Use Tiger," she calmly said whilst handing the toy over.

"Tiger?"

"Yes, that's Tiger."

"Named after Tiger Woods I presume."

"Exactly."

"I thought you didn't like golf."

"I don't. Whenever my husband watches golf, Tiger usually keeps me company."

"I thought that's why I was here."

"He may feel left out; we've been through a lot."

"I think he's retired from golf."

"That's why he's here."

"So where do you want Tiger?"

"I'll leave it for you two to work out."

She then turned onto her elbows and stuck out her bum as I kneeled for a moment looking at Tiger before reaching down to my trousers and removing a lubricant packet from my jeans, applying some to Tiger's head. It seemed logical Tiger was to go into the smaller hole, as I had only played golf five times or so and he was a world champion. I assisted Tiger for the hole in one before taking my own putt, moving slowly for a few minutes then picking up the pace, forcing the palm of my hand to one of her cheeks a few times whilst juggling Tiger with the other. We became a married couple playing out the monthly get together, lost at sea on a raft during a love storm. I had to dismount and change the coat as the rain became heavier, but it seemed I had gone back into it unprepared. I wasn't in need of a raincoat; I was more in need of a pair of flippers and a snorkel. The storm showed no sign of calming, and we played out several survival tactics before eventually escaping, both laid back on a small deserted island where we could catch our breath, surprised we came out alive.

After the heartbeats had slowed down, our clothes went on just as quickly as they'd come off. Followed by a fortunate amount of cash, and an unfortunate exchange of goodbyes, I left, making my way to the hotel entrance where I stood for a while outside. I lit up a cigarette, standing with a smile on my face, looking around at everything in a different way. Moments over money was always my life approach, mainly because money was hardly around, but this time it felt like I had both. The weight on my head had shifted right down to my feet, anchoring me to the floor, allowing my neck to rise, observing the race as opposed to being a part of it. And for the first time in twenty-eight years visiting the city, I noticed the beauty it held and I embraced all of it.

Good old London. A town where everyone rushes around excited to be anywhere, partaking in the ever-lasting marathon where the feeling of winning happens every day. Eager to wake each morning and even more grateful to be besides hundreds of strangers, embracing a moment of civilisation that thousands of dead relatives had worked hard to form. Sipping away on hot drinks made from beans grown in a foreign land, to energise our minds and help fulfil the week's potential, followed by a weekend of champagne celebrations in honour of doing it. A wonderful appreciation of living repeated week after week, year after year, enriching our souls until we find ourselves slouched in the corner of a room, surrounded by family, sharing our stories with grandchildren, of which they ask: what happened next? And we say: it's time to sleep now children, but when you wake I shall continue the story. Then we sit back sipping cognac in contentment, becoming witness to many moments of family continuing to enjoy the good times.

I even began walking at a pace I'd never done, a new walk for a new me. It wasn't slow yet it felt like everyone was passing me, as if I was driving a classic mini in a race on a formula one track. In my head, it was just right. I was in a nice car and cruising, enjoying the ride, not the speed. My favourite song then came into my head. I continued to stroll for a good mile, enjoying the vibrations of my high, singing out softly with my teeth showing.

"You got a fast car
I want a ticket to anywhere
Maybe we can make a deal
Maybe together we can get somewhere
Any place is better
Starting from zero got nothing to lose"

I ended back in the square where the previous night had concluded, where the choice of drinking establishments was plentiful. I stood for a moment and spun around like I was in my old work chair, looking at all the bars surrounding me. Two for one cocktail and flashing happy hour neon signs. One building called out to me more than the others. It being a week of new experiences, I was drawn to it, so throwing off all indecision, I made my way in.

[8]

A hidden environment should surprise you once you reach the main floor. I stood scoping this place as my opinion of it all came together. It was nothing like sitting at home in my shorts, playing online with the laptop. I didn't think it would be busy for starters. It was like an underground football stadium. Every time I saw a scene in a film there were always only a few people, dressed elegantly around each gaming table. But this place was over-crowded. Men and women from all over the world, all walks of life, clothes from charming to charity. All surrounding each table and standing behind the gamblers, a queue of desperate, greedy risk-takers awaiting their chance to get a look-in at lady luck. The noise was something else. Hundreds of languages echoed at once, moulding a loud Neanderthal-like mumble together with the sound of coloured poker chips clapping as they ran impatiently through the punter's hands. Plastic money had replaced paper, each value a specific colour, which made it easy to spot the rich from the poor or, winners from losers.

[Text message]
From: London's Calling
How did it go?

[Text message]
To: London's Calling
Was fun.

[Text message]
From: London's Calling
Nice. Are you still in the city?

[Text message]
To: London's Calling
Yes.

[Text message]
From: London's Calling
A bar?

[Text message]
To: London's Calling
No, casino.

[Text message]
From: London's Calling
Which one?

[Text message]
To: London's Calling
********** casino

I needed a few drinks after eating everything up. The bar was facing me from way over the other side of the room. I felt like a penguin looking for the mate and offspring as I squeezed and dodged through the seekers and players. Every so often one jumped back from a table in anger or excitement, the odd time bomb that made the journey seem like I was in a spider's web. At the bar I ordered the usual alcoholic beverage for when I've passed the tipsy mark, sat on a stool as the company of my "fuck buddy" was still strong, and looked out to the floor for a while as the anarchy unfolded.

"Can I sit?"

I looked up to see a glowing lady in her early forties dressed in a glittering silver frock and silver earrings. Her smooth shiny skin seemed due to a cream with a strong oaky scent.

"Sure." I replied innocently.

She sat on the stool with her body facing me, a bright smile, her blonde curly hair paying favour to a confident presence.

"Are you here alone?"

"I am."

"I'm Alexandra."

She held out a folded palm. I touched her fingers and gently shook them.

"Benjamin."

"Hello Benjamin."

"Where are you from?" I asked

"Originally Hungary."

"Nice."

"Have you been?"

"I haven't."

"So what are your plans for the evening Benjamin?"

"No plans."

"Do you work in the city?"

"Sometimes."

"What do you do?"

"I'm currently in between jobs."

"Did you come here from work?"

"No, just a spontaneous night."

"A little overdressed for a spontaneous night, you must have had some intentions in mind."

"Like what?"

"Meet a nice young girl maybe."

"Nope."

"Do you have a girlfriend?"

"I'm in between girlfriends too."

"I see." She smiled, looking behind for the barman, holding her finger up. He strolled over.

"Gin and tonic please."

"Are you here with your husband?"

"No. I came to meet someone but they let me down."

"So, you are also alone and a little overdressed."

"It seems so."

"Do you work in the city?"

"I do yes."

"Which part?"

"All over. But I come here often."

"Do you gamble?"

"No, but my friends do."

"So you are their lucky charm."

"Something like that."

We shared a stare over our drinks, after which I placed my attention on the water hole and thirsty gamers. Two young ladies appeared, about to cross my view of the floor, both dressed in outfits that displayed more flesh than material. I made eye contact and exchanged smiles as they passed. Alexandra had noticed me looking.

"Why don't you go and talk to them?"

"Who?"

"Who? The two girls you couldn't take your eyes and teeth off."

"HAHAHAHA maybe later."

"You know sex won't kill you, but chasing it will. You should put that energy into something else. And not only will you achieve more, you will have a lot of girls coming to you."

"You're smart aren't you?"

"Smart? Well, in some areas, like running a business and getting what I want, but I'm not really educated, I never went into school much."

"Me neither. Well, I mean I did go in but I wasn't really there, if you get what I mean."

"I do."

"I wish I tried more though. It helps to get a better job, a better job gets you better money, and you need money to do things in this world."

"And that was exactly my problem. I wanted to get away, explore different countries and ways of living. I had all the time in the world but no money to see it. But if you want something, really want something, you'll find a way."

"So have you travelled?"

"Over fifty countries and counting."

"Wow."

"Well. It was lovely meeting you Benjamin, but I have just noticed another friend and must go and say hello."

She stood, and again held her palm and fingers out. I shook them.

"Nice to meet you Alexandra."

I watched Alexandra approach a gentleman, place an arm around him, kissing him on the cheek. He handed her some plastic chips. I then took my sight from the floor and aimed it more at the interior of the building. There were neither clocks nor windows, so the sight and sign of time had disappeared, a house tactic I assumed. I sat for a while in the same place and watched the crowds slowly break away. Once I had reached my fifth drink, the temptation to go closer to the tables was getting harder to resist. I ordered my sixth and walked over to one of the blackjack tables, my drunken wobble helping me that time dodge the time bombs with ease. I started to feel I was fitting in nicely. I took an empty seat and players box at a table, waiting for the hand to finish, then found myself in a somewhat awkward position with the dealer. He was holding an unflinching stare towards me. I thought it was because of my intoxicated state, so I stared back without blinking, hoping he would excuse me.

"Are you going to play sir?"

"Please, ok… can," I attempted.

I decided to let my actions do the talking, took some paper money from my pocket and held it out to him. He tapped on the table insisting I placed the money there, a rule I had learnt, being that you can't have any, bar eye contact, with a dealer. He counted out seventy-five pounds. In return, I received three plastic chips. It was a tenth of what the others had, but it was fine, they could tell I was new, and I could tell they could tell. They all gave the same sympathetic smile whilst they patiently waited.

"Place your bets," the dealer said carelessly.

Honestly, it was like being at a funeral. Having received the benefit of the doubt for being there so short a time, I decided to give the benefit of the doubt to someone who had clearly been there too long. I decided to enjoy the moment. Everyone had already placed their bets before I had handed over the money, so it was just on me to act. I placed all three of my chips down, letting everyone know I knew what I was doing; trying to gain back some of the pride I had lost.

The dealer began placing down cards in front of everyone playing; the cards flew around the table so fast I didn't know where to look. It reminded me of a time I was on holiday as a teen on a nude beach amongst fifty young ladies. I woke up the next day with whiplash. The sound of the dealer spilling out numbers like an auctioneer also added to the distraction. Before I could even process anything, it was on me to either stick on my hand or ask for another card to help get closer to twenty-one. I had a king and a six, a total of sixteen, and the dealer's showing card was an eight so it seemed logical to take another. As I did so, I took my focus away from the table to pick my drink up from the side unit beside me, only to return to see there were no longer any cards in front of me, or any chips. I then watched the dealer deal himself a four, and then a nine; with his eight already he had made a total of twenty-one, beating everyone on the table. He snatched everyone's chips away as well as my smile, now placed on his own face. We all frowned and shook our heads in disbelief. He looked at me with a smirk before placing the chips in his little tray. I walked away with what little pride I had and swayed to the exit, making a drunken but solid promise to myself never to return again.

[9]

I woke the following morning with a subtle smile on my face and a confused thought in my mind, adding further difficulty to the identity and memory piecing. The thought as to why my alarm was still shaking me awake when I didn't have anything to get up for. I was certain I had turned it off. Or maybe just thought about turning it off and never did.

The effects of never being fully asleep and never fully awake are such that conscious and subconscious marry, and I'm faced with the constant struggle in separating my intentions from my actions, my thoughts and what was said, forever trying to remember my movements and frequently repeating my words.

I hit the off button and rolled onto my back, this time only holding the subtle smile on my face. I felt calm. Relaxed not rushed. I even felt the need to rekindle working out. I remembered my muscles for once, when usually they remembered me. It had been a while and seemed the right thing to do, especially if I planned to keep Benjamin Joy alive. I did however crave the devil's milk, and a can beside me caught my eye. I was amazed at how I could remember to leave myself something, despite forgetting most other things. I guessed it was another form of muscle memory. I decided to compromise. Work out for an hour, the reward being the can of beer, an incentive as such. Two things I didn't feel went hand in hand though, something I would never advise anyone else copy. But in the state I was in, I saw it as a step forward, and taking small steps is something I would always advise. The workout lasted half an hour. I sat back in a sweat that would be very appealing for a dog to lick, but also deadly as it was mostly alcohol that seeping through. I no longer saw the can of beer as a reward but more a forfeit. I began sipping. Where there's a will there's an explanation. One can turned into two, and then two shortly turned into a trip to the shop where I also picked up some vegetables and meat and cooked a nutritious meal. It felt like a vacation. Every hour filled its worth, a lazy day watching some movies and sipping a few beers with several short siestas in between.

[Text message]
From: London's Calling
Ready to go again?

[Text message]
To: London's Calling
Yes.

[Text message]
From: London's Calling
8pm
2 hours
a couple
****** hotel.

[Text message]
To: London's Calling
A couple? As in two women?

[Text message]
From: London's Calling
No, man and woman, no touch with man and more money.

[Text message]
To: London's Calling
Ok.

[Text message]
From: London's Calling
Wait in the bar, order yourself a drink.

I arrived on the dot and entered the hotel's small lobby. Right away I could see to my left a tavern-like room, and naturally made my way through. I approached the bar that was lined from one end to the other with empty red stools. The walls were also red and faced black dining tables and leather Chesterfield type chairs fit for thirty guests. All neatly composed and facing a pianist, who was playing a classical smooth paced tune. The room was relaxed; three waitresses moving delicately around the space like polite mice making sure the cool cats were looked after. I ordered a pint of beer at the bar and then chose one of the tables in plain view to the entrance so I could be noticed. I signalled my arrival and calmly sipped my beer and waited. Informed the couple were not so calm, I assumed I was going to be sitting for a while. I used the moment to swallow my fuck buddy, remembering to break it in half before enjoying my time down in the bar whilst nerves were mending in a room above.

Half way through my beer, a middle-aged man approached the bar entrance, his eyes fixated on me. A slow slouched walk I took as a sign that the night would be over quicker than I could finish my beer. I stood to greet him and we gripped hands and exchanged names before sitting. A waitress then appeared from nowhere, a Houdini in reverse. She offered her services delivering drinks and the guy took to it confidently.

"I will have the same as him," he said, pointing to my beer.

He then sat back in his chair with his hands held together, making one big fist between his legs, an uptight-seated position that made me question if he had been sent down with the company of a butt plug. I could feel his nerves, and for some reason my being calm seemed to agitate him.

"We are very nervous."

"That's ok. It's normal. Is it your first time?"

"Yes," he said with a sincere smile. "Where we are from people don't even approach one another in discos."

"What made you want to do it?"

"I guess we are more open than most people, where we are from anyway. We thought it could be something different, exciting, more suitable for us. We're just a little nervous."

"I'm sure you will feel more at ease, there's no rush, but maybe not too long otherwise your partner may fall asleep."

"I think she's too nervous to fall asleep."

I chuckled, but by the look on his face he wasn't trying to add any humour, so I eased down to a smile whilst picturing his wife sitting upstairs with more than her hands clenched, which forced me to chuckle again. The waitress delivered his beer and we both raised our glasses in a formal manner, took a sip followed by a moment of silence before I continued my examination.

"Is it your first time in London?"

"No. I have been many times but only to visit. We moved here last month as I was offered a job. Well, it is with the same company, just a different position and of course a different location."

"Oh, so you live here now?"

"We do."

"What kind of work do you do, if you don't mind my asking?"

He began explaining and I sat nodding my head in between sips of beer. It seemed I had chosen the right topic, as he was a lot more comfortable. Unlatching his hands and even dropping his shoulders, sinking his body down into the seat. So much so, it removed the butt plug. Things were running smoothly now. It felt like we were old college friends out for an overdue catch-up and had both forgotten why we were there. I then asked a couple of questions about his partner to reel it back in, even somehow get an idea of her appearance. "Love has no face," as Will said. Whilst the capitalist, con artists shake the spear of attraction at us, removing a true meaning and replacing it with a vision that pairs love with beauty and money. I felt I had outgrown that and usually kept the many pre-set judgements suppressed. Every now and then one managed to creep in though. I would agree with William, but this man was sharply dressed, well-groomed, had money. The money makes the assumption, as I had no idea what he was talking about with his job. A unique skill often pays more, it all made me feel he was a man of the encoded way, thus confident his partner would be attractive and that I was in for yet another easy ride.

"Is there anything you would like to run by me, boundaries as such?" I suggested, moving up to the room without suggesting moving up to the room because my fuck buddy had started to drain blood from my brain.

"If we can restrain from any kissing on the lips, that would be good." He replied.

Most would find it odd and see sex more the unforgiving action. I've also felt kissing as the plug and fuel that can spark a flame, start the heart beating faster than usual. The closed-eyed and free from thought-moment where we seek and hope cupid is passing and we get to sense that arrow fill our bodies with the hard to explain feeling of ecstasy. So that the kiss being removed merely left a physical connection, meaningless, and as I wasn't looking for a relationship it suited me just fine. Especially if there was no attraction. It was a win-win, and so I simply replied:

"Of course."

"Great. Shall we go up?"

"Yes let's."

We both stood and made our way to the lift. My bad timing of the fuck buddy was forcing me to throw my leg out with each step, followed by placing my hand in my pocket and applying a barrier. When we reached the room all I could smell was alcohol in the air. It was like wine was the scent of an air freshener and someone had mascaraed the room with four cans of it. The entrance was small, almost like an oversized cloakroom with even a fancy coat holder and a small table with a large bowl placed in the centre. We made our way to a large room that was separated from the cloakroom by wooden framing and doors that opened out into the bedroom. Two large Mr and Mrs beds owned the space, separated by a shared side table that homed a large lamp. There was also a large sofa that sat by the window, attended by a golden-framed unit with a glass top and a large chest of drawers against the wall opposite. Many empty bottles of wine were lined up on the drawers, surprising to see as the husband didn't seem drunk at all. I would have been on the tipsy mark myself at that amount of intake. It was soon clear the wife was the main culprit and the husband only an accessory or witness. She even managed to fall during our greet, which would have been normal and expected if she was standing, but she was sat down on one of the beds. She was very attractive, petite with a sense of innocence. Curly blonde hair and a tight body that fitted well in her black silk nighty with matching underwear; a dress that was quite long but showed some skin, allowing room for my imagination. That excited me. The kind of seductive lingerie you'd get in the eighties. It was refreshing in comparison to the dental floss I was used to seeing. Her maturity was sexy and would have been a lot more if the teenage binge was removed from her, but it was clear it was needed.

"I'm very nervous," she said with a nervous giggle.

"Yes I heard. I would be more concerned if you weren't. Most people are, to begin with, so it's ok."

"That's good to hear," her nervous giggle continued.

I decided at that point to relax and sit down on the same bed as her on the opposite end, hoping my being comfortable would cut some tension and help her relax. The husband poured and handed me a glass of wine, then sat on the other bed facing us.

"Are you ok?" he said to his partner in a subtle whisper and smile.

"Yes," she replied with nervous eyes and a matching smirk.

"Do you want to carry on?" he aimed at her with growing eyes.

She looked over toward me. I couldn't help but make eye contact before addressing my attention to my glass of wine, using my peripheral vision to acknowledge her response.

"Yes," she whispered whilst nodding, focused on the husband before glancing over at me.

The husband then went into a slouched, forward position, his hands back to one big fist. We found ourselves in a circle of silence. It was like three cars had approached a roundabout at the same time waiting for someone to make the first move. A neutral position where the couple made eye contact with one another followed by a light laugh where air was pushed through their nostrils. I made eye contact with the husband, whilst enjoying my wine, before I felt both pairs of eyes on me. The husband looked at his wife and then back at me, and I looked over at the wife and she looked over to her husband, which led the husband to ask:

"So how do you think we should start?"

"Well, I think you two should start, relax a bit, and then I will join in when I see fit."

The husband immediately took the right of way, approached his wife and parked up beside her. The roundabout in motion, I also went into gear and moved over to his old space, making some room for them. Being a woman driving under the influence, it was expected that her manoeuvres would take longer than usual before another parking spot opened up. So I just went back into neutral, continued sipping my wine and watched on. A few minutes passed and nothing seemed to be moving forward, so I removed my seat belt, stood and began removing my shirt. This caught their attention, although more so the wive's. She sat up slightly and watched, starting on my body as I popped a button, followed by a serious stare into my eyes during the small gap in between as I moved to the next one. To and fro, until my shirt was fully removed. She then drifted toward me and began assisting with removing my belt and trousers, pulling down my boxers and taking to me confidently, like a monkey grabbing its next branch. She attempted to place it into her mouth but it kept hitting her cheek, I assumed because she saw double. After three attempts she managed to put it in. The husband had some difficulty with his branch. At this moment, it looked more like a modelling, party-balloon, and he was stretching it out so he could later perform and shape a sword, once he had overcome his nerves. I went onto the bed and laid on my back as she continued. The husband stood at the bottom where he collided with the drawers, rattling the empty wine bottles, a slight distraction but I guess he stood there for a better view. A nice sight for him but not so much for me as I couldn't help but notice him. My head was raised on the

106

pillow and it was a strain to look downwards. It didn't last long though as she soon came up for air and began removing her dress, blocking my view of any deflated balloons and replacing it with her filled ones. She then began to remove her underwear as I addressed my safety precautions, after which she climbed onto me with her back fully stretched and shifting straight into fifth gear, which lasted a good five seconds. I assumed it would only be a matter of time in her state before she would crash, her airbags saving us both from head injuries. The speed then slowed right down, we were more intimate. The husband made progress with his sword and noticing a free but tight spot he rapidly approached and attempted to get into it, but it seemed the tyre still needed more air. As we continued, her face was very close to mine; our lips only separated by the air that pushed out from her mouth, caused by each one of her pelvic thrusts. The closeness and the fact I held her face and head with both my hands made it almost impossible not to go in for a kiss. I felt like a fly that had landed on a windscreen dodging the wiper. I decided to release her head to gain some distance, where I then caught the questioning gaze from the husband through the sandhills created each time she raised up. It snapped me out of it and I held back.

That moment had been erased but another stronger one was en route. The closeness held a definite physical connection, but it seemed the unlatching and new distance had caused a mental one. Our eyes locked, exchanging rays of energy that heightened a conscious focus. I had a more sensitive awareness of her moving up and down on me. We may have dodged cupid's arrow, but he had returned, this time with his gun. Shooting her in the back and piercing right through and hitting my chest, causing her to go into shock. She began shaking and squeezing the life out of me. We both survived the bullet, but the atmosphere was surely killed. Even though the husband was unaware of what occurred with us he had again lost the life of his dagger and was back performing reviving procedures. I tapped her thigh a couple of times with the palm of my hand and she climbed off to help the husband with his resuscitation, offering her mouth, whilst I took a minute to get myself together and enjoy a few more sips of wine as well as discarding the evidence of our moment of lust.

The great thing about a fuck buddy is not just that they are able to assist nature but they also defy it. In a natural situation, I assume all men experience. During the act there tends to be a river of meaningful promises constantly flowing into the ear of your loved one, all the way up until the tadpoles have swum to the departing ship. After which one can't help but feel the need to join them and get as far away as possible. A conflict between instinct and the mind, comfort or consent to leave, causing the man to walk around in circles of confusion as the general clocks off from his night watch and tucks up into bed. My instincts were the same, but with a fuck buddy the general is eager to put in overtime. I only wished it could have been passed on to the husband as he continued to be unfit to work, which must have brought some distress to the wife as she turned to me and said somewhat frustrated.

"Do you mind if you sit back for a while?"

"No, not at all."

"I'm just not used to being around men," the husband said embarrassed.

"Sure. I'm not here," I replied whilst pouring some more wine.

"Ok," he whispered and smirked.

I re-filled my glass and sat amongst the shadows in the corner of the room, continuing to sip. The husband climbed onto the bed as the wife walked over to a large duffle type bag removing a large wooden panel and some kind of rag. The husband then went onto all fours as the wife stuffed his mouth with the rag before standing adjacent to him and sizing up her aim with the wooden panel to his backside. She then took the first strike, creating a large sound that rebounded off the walls followed by the husband's mumbled scream.

"Are you a pathetic man?" The wife screamed into his ear before retaking her position behind him.

She then took another whack, this time with more force.

"Answer me!" she said again, screaming but keeping her position behind the husband.

"MMMMMMMMMMM!" A muffled groan roared from the husband.

I gazed through the open doors that separated the room looking for the wife as the woman in the room had completely changed.

"Look at Benjamin!" she said with her teeth gritted.

She then grabbed the husband's hair and forced his head over in my direction.

"Tell him you are pathetic!" she screamed into his ear.

She then struck his backside with the wooden panel, holding it in both hands.

"Tell him!" she continued to scream out.

"MMMM MMM MMMMM MM." Another longer muffle coming from the husband.

I watched jaw-dropped, holding my glass of wine millimetres from my lips as she continued striking him. At every whack I'd tense up, like I had adopted the butt plug the husband was sent down to the bar with. The pace sped up, as did the groans, continuing until he had relieved himself and fallen flat on the bed, the redness on his bum glowing like a brake light onto the ceiling. The wife then placed the panel back into the duffle bag whilst looking over at me, winking as if she just ran over some kind of animal and enjoyed it. She then moved closer to the bed, nearer to me and bent over, her taillight shining my way. I felt the sudden urge to walk over and introduce myself as dogs do for a while before retaking the safety measures. My engine restarted and I took the wheel again whilst she sat in the passenger seat. I started slow. Her bum pushed up against my waist with subtle but strong hits, which sounded like one audience member giving a single cupped clap. I then applied the gas, which then sounded like the rest of the audience joining in with the ovation. We drove on for a few miles, leaving the husband behind like road kill, laying face down on the bed. I didn't stop until I was on empty and provided the small amount of oil suggesting it would need topping up before driving again. The wine was no longer a lone smell. Sweat and steam mixed within the room. This followed by another moment of silence, or at least unspoken words as the sound of the wife's panting made noise. I finished my wine before getting dressed, after which I felt the only thing left to say was:

"Well. It was nice to meet you both, but I'm in desperate need of some nicotine."

They both accompanied me to the door where I received my driving tuition fee, a kiss from the wife and a farewell shake from my old college friend. Outside the hotel, I took out a cigarette and lit up, walking in the direction I came from. Maybe it was subconscious, or maybe it was the plan all along, but I ended up going to the one place I promised I would never go again.

[10]

It seemed gambling was always the intention. More so than anything else as I couldn't stop once I'd entered. Something had overcome me. I was already familiar with the layout and didn't care to find a clock; there was no time to look around and no time for hesitation. Not even time to go to the bar; although I knew you could order drinks at the table, I put it behind my first intention. I no longer felt like a penguin moving through the crowd and dodging the time bombs either. I was cool and collected and danced through the spider's web like a rhythmic gymnast, the cash already in my hand acting as the piece of ribbon, ready to throw down and exchange for the plastic. As I approached a blackjack table someone got up to leave, like I was expected, and they were merely keeping the chair warm until my arrival. I took a seat and placed the cash straight down onto the table without looking at the dealer, making everyone aware that I was aware of the no hand-over rule. As I took care of one rule, another hit me. I took out my phone whilst awaiting the chip exchange and was approached by another staff member who asked me to put it away. Another instruction clearly everyone else knew, but I convinced myself otherwise. I assumed even the professionals would forget that one, or pretend to anyway, so it didn't count. I resumed my original, confident state.

I swapped two hundred pounds, more than I wanted to but there was no way I was going to announce it. Eight chips, each valuing twenty-five pounds. I placed half of them down for the first hand. I then awaited the dealer before I took a look at him. I knew this way his eyes would be focused on laying down the cards, avoiding contact with mine. This way I could complete my aim of getting a feel for his energy. I made my glance after the first hand was out and was caught off guard. My expectations of a miserable 'he' was confronted by an attractive 'she'. I held my gawk up until it was on me to decide what I wanted to do with my hand. Looking right into my eyes and smiling before raising her eyebrows and frowning, a suggestive hurry up face, which excited me and messed up my focus. Damn, that place was sneaky. I moved my eyes from hers and looked down to become even more excited. If lady luck was ever to appear, I'm sure that is what she would look like. The queen of hearts. It seemed she had brought along her twin sister for the night, as I had two. I split the hand, which cost me the remaining half of my stack as I was playing two hands, but it gave me the chance to double my money. It wasn't long until the twins, lady and luck were paired with jacks making me have two hands of twenty, looking strong against the dealer's potential. She had a six on show and would need to draw two more cards, a higher risk of going over twenty-one. Once everyone was done, she dealt her second card, which turned out to be a king, making sixteen. So as expected, a third was to follow, seeing as she was below seventeen, and it turned out to be a charming ten, making twenty-six. Everyone had won at the table, and I had won twice, doubling my money as well as regaining my pride from the previous night. I asked the dealer if a waitress could be called so I could continue drinking whilst playing. I'd decided to up the wager and placed two hundred pounds down on one hand, now more interested in the money than the dealer. I concentrated more on my decisions, playing the odds, going on to win five hands in a row before losing one. I walked away from the table carrying my chips and unknown profit straight to the cashier. I cashed out an even twelve hundred and made my way over to the bar where I would endure the madness and again made the promise never to gamble. I had walked away in the green and could go on to say I had beaten the house.

I paid for my drink with a twenty-pound note and let the barman keep the change. After sharing a respectful head nod with him I turned to observe the floor. Deja vu. The two girls from the night prior began approaching, about to cross my view again, and this time, after the exchange of eyes and smiles, I stepped out and began breaking the ice.

"If you two are going to be here all week to block my view can you let me know now so I can change my seat?"

They both stopped and stared at one another, then toward me with blank looks. Neither had a clue what I meant. Their stares even made me forget what I meant. But a first line is always hit or miss. It was certainly a miss.

"You were both here last night, right?"

"Yeah," one of the girls said still holding a confused expression.

"And I was sitting here."

"Really?" the other responded, also holding the confused expression on her face.

We stood awkwardly for a moment. I felt I should try my luck and change the game of approach to a normal civilised situation.

"Do you have boyfriends?"

"Yes." they both replied in the exact same time and tone.

Of course they did. Even when they don't, most always say they do, and this time I was expecting the response. A textbook response that simply tests a man's confidence. Where many would just uncomfortably walk away thinking it was the end when really it can be an invitation, depending on the behaviour of the body. In this case it was unguarded with no sign of rushing off anywhere. I continued.

"Just the one or…?" I continued with a subtle smirk.

Again they stared, accompanied with subtle smiles, this time understanding but hesitant to respond. A subtle witty remark where I was clearly complementing them, mingled with the offering and a test of personality.

"One obviously," the one standing closest snatched at me.

Of course obviously. I understood admitting to seeing more than one-person projects a negative attitude, which no one wants to portray, especially to the person providing the one thing more addictive than all substances combined. Attention!

"What are your names?"

"I'm Stacey and this is Lacy."

"Hello Stacey, hello Lacy."

"What's yours?" Lacy said whilst taking a peek, and a judgement, at my shoes.

"Joy. Benjamin Joy."

I felt like one of James Bond's sons. Despite them never becoming known to the silver screen, it made sense he would have many offspring. Although it's also more likely he would produce mostly girls due to a womanising lifestyle, ironic karma as such, great. That's another thirty more girls with exceedingly high one-way unconditional expectation issues. Nice one Dad.

"We're going to sit upstairs. Do you want to come Benjamin?"

"Sure."

I followed behind as they lead me to a staircase where we would soon sit at a high table close to a balcony. We ordered cocktails, (and no mine wasn't a Martini) as well as some shots, where shortly after Lacy decided to question my ability to sustain. I went to give a modest answer, but she interrupted by stating:

"I bet I could drink you under the table."

I smirked and glared for a while. Despite 'bet' being a good choice of word for our setting, the others were not so good to hear. It was the first time I had really thought about that and actually become aware of my habit. After hearing someone make that statement, I felt they weren't even close to where I was. A place that holds no proud feeling, one where you would certainly never feel like reciting that phrase to anyone. I was used to the top of the table being the floor, and the ability to be under it meant something darker. I felt no need to announce all of that,

116

but also didn't want to encourage anything. I simply smiled and said.

"Yes".

"I have a question!" Stacey said with a spring in her back.

"Make it a good one, Stacey," I announced with a frown.

"Where is your dream holiday destination?"

Lacy jumped in before I could even think.

"Barbados!"

"Oh my god, mine too!" Stacey squealed and I was left out of the conversation.

"Really? Shall we go?"

"Definitely. Will you come with us Ben? Do you like Benjamin or Ben?"

"Either," I replied wide-eyed.

"What was your last name again?"

"Joy."

"Ooh, BJ."

They began laughing like hyenas. The cocktails and shots flowed and we began flirting, first with alcohol, then with one another. It wasn't long before I had a short visit from the drop phase. I lifted my drink to take a sip that took longer than usual as I was holding back my own laugh caught from the girls giggling, but what it was all about I couldn't say. It then went quiet as I sipped my drink and closed my eyes. I then placed my drink back down and opened my eyes only to see the two of them passionately kissing. I looked around to see if anyone else was watching, not because I was so much shocked or embarrassed by their actions but because I thought it was a nice sight, and I wanted to see if others thought the same.

"Let's go and play roulette!" Stacey said, dragging Lacy and me by the arms.

I grabbed my glass with my free arm, finishing off the dregs before we began making our way back down to the main floor. Beside the table, at the exact moment I took money from my pocket, I was approached with the drop phase. This time it wasn't going anywhere. The last thing I saw and heard was my feet and the sound of a closing door.

[11]

I woke soaked in sweat, which caused me to shoot up as if I had hit the snooze button one too many times and was late for work. I looked around. Before my brain could tell me my name, or what had happened, the first question was my whereabouts. It was clearly a hotel room. I noticed dents in the pillow beside me that suggested someone else had slept there, but with no suggestion as to whom. A small bottle of vodka that seemed to be from the room's minibar sat on the bedside table next to me. I shot it down just as quick as I had shot up, the burn attacking my throat, then my head, causing my body to shut down and fall back to the pillow.

I laid with the bottom of my palms pushed into my eyes, attempting to recollect. The main question was where my money went. I moved over to the side of the bed and reached down for my jeans to check the pockets. I had more than I remembered from the blackjack winnings. It took another minute to remember playing roulette. Stacey and Lacy were with me. I remembered another winning streak, betting on red because of the girls, I mentioned lust was the night's genre and it came in four times in a row, doubling the money I had already doubled.

Before I could remember anything else the toilet in the en suite flushed. I watched the bathroom door, nervously awaiting the person to show a face. The room was dark so I had to keep adjusting my head, squinting to catch the light that bounced within the room. A silhouette began walking towards me. It was Alexandra, glowing as usual and wrapped in a towel, which she dropped when she reached the bottom of the bed, displaying her toned and busty frame.

"How are you feeling Benjamin?"

She took some cream out from her bag on the floor and began applying it to her body. I sat up and began twiddling my finger with the bed sheet to avoid staring.

"Not so great, how are you?"

"Take a cold shower you'll feel better," she said as she continued to cream her legs.

My thoughts hit a brick wall. Four empty condom wrappers on the floor beside me caught my eye, suggesting a lot but without a single vision. Another good night and the climax stored away in a lost property box.

"What time did we get here?"

"Around 3 am."

"What happened?"

"You don't remember?"

"I remember being with Stacey and Lacy at the casino."

"Ahh. Well, I had to intrude on your little party otherwise they'll never learn. Still acting like civilians and dropping their pants for free drinks and a little flash of the money."

"And us?"

"Us what?"

"What did we get up to?"

"You don't remember?"

"No."

"Do you drink a lot?"

"No."

"We had some fun."

I laid back down and again placed the palm of my hands into my eye sockets.

"The night we met, George had told me where to find you. George is good in some areas, but you didn't really think he was the brain behind my business."

"So the guy at the casino that night, he was a client?"

"He was."

"So you are a sex worker?"

"I have regular clients but I don't sleep with any."

"How do you manage that?"

"Experience. Wealthy men care more about appearance than sex. I'm like a sports car you can take indoors. I sleep with whom I choose. Knowing your self-worth and valuing your time will take you further. I suggest you should remember that if you wish to continue this line of work."

"So this was like a test?"

"A little."

"What?"

"Well a little for Performance yes. Before I can be sure which clients of mine I allow you to meet and also because a woman still has an itch to scratch, despite being passed my prime"

"So how did I do?"

"Go and take a cold shower."

I picked my clothes up from the floor and headed to the en suite to shower and shine my teeth. I stood over the basin looking at my tiresome, hung over features in the mirror. With the drop phase erasing any recollection, and knowing I was being tested for performance, I decided to work myself up. My morning glory started to unravel the towel from around my waist, dropping it to my feet. I did worry for a moment that it may come across somewhat impolite to go back into the room all guns blazing, but being that she seemed comfortable to be naked around me I felt it couldn't mean anything more than suggestive. I took a deep breath and left the bathroom fully extended, like a pirate's telescope between my legs, ready to scope out the treasures. After a double scan with the scope, I was left spying on an empty room, brightened from the drawn curtains, highlighting a perfectly made bed. The only female quality present being the flowered wallpaper. Alexandra had vacated whilst I was in the shower.

Checking out before I could check-in. And so I had entered a room more frustrated than when I had left it. I couldn't help but laugh about it while dressing, which took longer than usual. I got there in the end, eventually making my way back to the cold walls and a cold can of the devil's piss from the fridge. I sat on my bed and began sipping with just enough energy to lift it to my mouth.

[Text message]
To: Peach
How are you?

[Text Message]
From: Peach
I'm ok, how are you?

[Text Message]
To: Peach
I'm fine.

Gabby knew what I was up to. I mean not everything, but she knew the bits in between, it wasn't new to her. She knew my next move before I did. And it wasn't like I didn't want to ask to go and see her at the time, I just didn't have the energy. I saw it then as only settling, just like my previous relations. Settling amongst the dark dust knowing it would only blow up again. I didn't like or want that, not with Gabby, the two doors we all tend to face at some point in our lives.

Door number one, where we walk through together and continue a toxic relationship because it holds a certain comfort that we fear we'll never find again. Mainly due to insecurities, where we pass responsibility to those we call our other half, the responsibility to provide love, thinking it will help with self. The problem is being that way will only ever attract a partner with the same motive, where give and take remains half full.

The second door we both walk through alone, go separate ways. Forever blaming the other and convincing ourselves and our allies that it's not that soul mates don't exist, it's just that one wasn't it. And we continue our quest in a delusional mind-set, replaying the same late-night talks and dinners with someone new, getting out most of the truth, with some white lies about our past. The main goal is to relate, leading up to the physical test, passing it adequately - it can always be worked on, until things become difficult and ordinary again; meet sleep and repeat.

It was the first time Gabby and I had approached door number one. It wasn't us, and I had to be cautious because I knew exactly where it could lead. A relation where door number one has been used consistently over the years, where your lives become formed from the pressures of society's expectations. You become trapped by marriage, mortgages or little munchkins. The contact of family and friends fade, as does the idea of doing it all again. So you stand side by side with your partner among other couples who also missed the boat home from Fantasy Island, where there seems to be more peace in a psychiatric ward.

Prides come together a few shameful times to celebrate birthdays, Christmas and other big days. Unoriginal and thoughtless gifts are exchanged whilst the room slowly clouds with secrets, lies and affairs. Oscar-worthy performances portraying the happy fulfilled life and battle between love birds fighting for the imaginary Romeo and Juliet award you may get to place in between your picture frames and overpriced vases on your ~~mindofpeace~~ mantelpiece.

124

Introductions and small talk, to begin with, accompanied by a few fake laughs before the sexes slowly magnet to opposite corners. Evenings fuelled by alcohol and drugs where the men rarely want it to end and the women's excitement usually partakes during the day of the night approaching and the getting ready part, which often peaks instantaneously to men forming a choir of laughter. Juliet drags Romeo home where they force themselves to make love, both fantasising about their old secret admirer or someone they saw that evening, using imagination to escape the reality. Making love continues to be breaking love, into many tiny pieces and becoming robotic instead of human, of which I mean intelligent enough to accept the love between one another has gone instead of pretending because you didn't embrace the moments nor face the truth. Just like the good memories of sleepless nights and exciting mornings during the Santa illusion. Golden medals of memories more valuable than any amount of money could have been won and kept as opposed to the taking part ribbon of regret constantly reminding you of a waste of time.

- Someone. Once

I decided to open up my laptop and make an effort looking for work. I knew I had to make money but the idea of working in my previous field and being miserable was too hard to settle for. After a short while I came across a company looking for creative content writers. It was an unpaid internship but I thought I could make money on the side and at least get my mind back to running the way it enjoyed. After applying I must have fallen asleep as I woke to the ping of my phone.

[Text message]
From: London's Calling
Are you free this evening?

I guess I had passed the test. Be careful what you wish for. And I often wished to be busy once, earning a sufficient amount, but I never actually realised it would be like this. I was exhausted, but also still in need of distraction and money.

[Text message]
To: London's Calling
I am.

[Text message]
From: London's Calling
Meeting is with another working girl, Scarlett.

[Text message]
To: London's Calling
Sure.

[Text message]
From: London's Calling
Hotel ***** Room 444 9pm
Meet Scarlett before you meet the client.

[Text message]
To: London's Calling
Will do.

[12]

I had made my way up to the fourth floor to wait for Scarlett, perched on a dark suede seat a few rooms down from the client. My body arched forward where my elbows and knees helped keep me stable. The surroundings were dark, maybe too dark. Black marbled walls and black carpet, neither capturing the firefly styled ceiling lights, where the glow just hovered. I remember sweat falling from my armpits down the side of my ribs, the excess of alcohol trying to get out and not in for once. There was also no sign of guests or any sounds from the rooms. It was quiet, so quiet my head soon dropped and I stared at the carpet where I couldn't work out if my eyes were open or closed. I just remember seeing nothing but shadows before a ding from the lift caused me to look up. A gold dress began approaching me. It was too hazy to see any other feature but as it floated closer it called out Benjamin, and I stood to put a face to the outfit.

"Yes," I said squinting, moving my head between the glowing.

"I've been waiting for you in the lobby for twenty minutes," she replied with gritted teeth.

"I thought it would be easier to meet you here."

"Well, you thought wrong!"

The dress twirled and began moving away from me. I'm sure Scarlett was a nice person, if you hadn't left her waiting, but she was clearly unimpressed and stormed ahead, making her way to the room where again her head and legs disappeared. I shadowed behind a flying dress. At the client's door she glanced at me before lifting her arm to knock. I caught her fist before any knowledge of our arrival was made known.

"Is there anything you want to discuss before we go in?" I whispered.

"No," she quickly replied in a normal tone.

She then re-attempted to knock and I caught her fist a second time.

"Just so I know if the client requests anything I can step in."

"This booking is for a performance right?" she said with a firm tone, her temper raising more with each word.

"Yeah," I replied, like a child being told off for backchat.

"And you were made aware of the play out?"

"No".

"Ok, so what will happen is we will get together, I will go down to assist you going up, and then any penetration I will either tuck to the side of me, or you can tuck it under me, on my belly, blocking any view from the client. Just do not put it in me."

"Right. But what if he comes closer?"

"If he requests anything that affects the way I work, I will make my own excuses myself, I have my own mouth."

She raised her arm and knocked on the door, again like an angry parent, Suddenly the room door opened, the light attacking us like the cave of wonders.

"Hello, come in, come in." A soft invitation from a gentleman.

I threw out my arm and palm and insisted Scarlett entered first. There wasn't much to the suite; it was bare, very clean and very bright with the scent of nicotine in the air.

"Just keep going down there. You will see the bedroom on the right."

We both continued to walk in search of the bedroom. The man followed after closing the door. The bedroom was darkened by the drawn curtains and only one lamp betrayed the presence of a large chair in the corner where an ashtray containing a burning cigarette rested on the arm. Scarlett sat on the bed, placing her clutch bag beside her. She removed her shoes, then some protection from her bag before she sat up on her knees awaiting the client. The routine seemed as natural to her as breathing, whereas I stayed close to her walking in small circles in a guarding like motion.

"So it's …" the client said whilst he pointed at Scarlett.

"Scarlett."

"Yes and Ben?"

"Yes."

"Awesome. I'm David. Would you both like a drink? I have wine or whisky."

"I'm fine thank you," Scarlett snapped out.

"I'll have a whisky please," I snapped out after.

"Sure, one whisky."

David began pouring me a drink and I shared a small stare with Scarlett, her face suggesting she wasn't happy with my choice, so I blinked a couple of times at her and then looked over at David. He was in his late thirties I'd say; short brown frizzy hair and a slim build with a polite persona. Once David handed me the whisky, he sat down in the chair a few metres from the bed. His face disappeared into the darkness and the glowing red from his cigarette could only be seen from the neck up.

"So I will leave it up to you two. Just do what you like," David suggested, as the red glow continued to grow.

Scarlett perched up and wobbled on her knees over to me and grabbed the hand holding the whisky. She attempted to pull it away but soon realised it was glued to me, causing her to tilt her head whilst looking into my eyes. I held my stare and glass until she looked away and let go. I could then tilt the glass to my mouth and finish it off before placing it down on the cabinet.

"Do you mind if I play with myself? Sorry, I thought I'd ask now to avoid any awkwardness," David said, leaning forward so his face could be seen.

"That's fine," Scarlett quickly answered for us both.

"As long as nothing comes flying my way David," I said jokingly, with a hint of seriousness.

"Of course." He chuckled as he vanished back into darkness.

I recomposed and turned to face Scarlett who had started crawling back to the headboard, simultaneously slipping the dress from her shoulders. I then walked to the base of the bed and began crawling onto it towards her whilst removing my shoes as she continued crawling back. Once we had found one another I went in for a kiss and she moved her head to the side, showing me her neck, so I began kissing her there before assisting her with removing the dress some more, then cupping her left breast with my hand and sucking on her nipple. A few seconds in some absurd heavy groaning began coming from David, causing myself and Scarlett to suddenly look at each other. We both smirked like school kids before trying to get back into the moment.

"I may need some assistance." I whispered into Scarlett's ear.

"What?" she replied in a normal tone.

Her tone caused me to look over at David, like a classroom scene where I wanted to see if the teacher had noticed us talking. Of course, I couldn't see his face, just a highlighted waist area the dim light from the lamp had then kindly pointed out for me. It made me even more shy down stairs.

"I need some help," I said with a suggestive downward look.

"Oh."

Scarlett sat up and placed me in her old position, took down my jeans and began slowly rubbing and then licking with a gentle tease whilst I removed my shirt. It didn't take long for me to become excited, after which Scarlett then positioned herself so she could show David what she was doing. She stared over toward him whilst she continued to massage me. The groans from the silhouette became deeper and heightened. After five minutes or so Scarlett opened up one of her condoms and placed it into her mouth before fitting it onto me and rolling it down with the tips of her fingers. She then climbed onto me but placing her body and the tip of me slightly away from the view of David, moving up and down whilst she held me in her palm against the outside of her stomach. Her poker face was glaring at mine for a moment before she tucked me away by her leg and placed her hands onto my chest, the illusion of intercourse still in full play. Things then sped up slightly and the sound of her bum hitting my thighs seemed to excite David. His low groans had changed to a high end pitch. Scarlett started to slow down and eventually climbed off me and bent over, facing David with a suggestive look in her eyes whilst looking at me with a frown, reminding me I was not welcome inside. As I positioned myself behind her David interrupted.

"Is it Ok if you do it from this side?"

"Sure," Scarlett said whilst spinning around, holding both her looks at me.

I crawled simultaneously to Scarlett's turn, my back now facing David. I tucked myself passed entry towards her belly button and she let out a subtle moan to indicate entry. I began thrusting and Scarlet continued to act whilst

David continued to sing, a harmony, both in sync with their groans. It wasn't long before David's groan overpowered Scarlett's and I gritted my teeth, looking down at my hands that were placed on both her cheeks, wishing I could cover my ears to avoid the large exhale of air that came from behind me. And just like that it was over.

"Thank you that was great," David said, taking out another cigarette.

Scarlett perked up like she just heard the school bell, grabbing her things and entering the en suite just beside us. I was only just removing the empty condom before getting dressed, when I turned to find David standing close to me.

"How long have you been doing this for?" he said, placing the cigarette into his mouth and creating a cloud of smoke.

"Not long, but long enough I guess."

"You have a nice body."

"Thanks."

"Would you like another drink?"

"Yes please."

David began pouring me a drink, the cigarette tucked in the side of his mouth and adding more clouds to the room.

"Are you allowed to smoke in here?" I enquired.

"Not really, but I always sleep with the windows open," he replied, handing me the whisky.

"I do the same thing."

The toilet flushed in the en suite and seconds later Scarlett was back in the room looking as fresh as when I had met her.

"Right, I need to go as I have someone waiting," she said through a fake smile.

"Sure," David acknowledged.

He took some money from a safe and handed it to Scarlett. She counted it quicker than a machine.

"Great, thank you, see you soon," she said hugging him and kissing him on the cheek.

"Bye Benjamin."

And she brushed passed me and left before I could even say goodbye, leaving only a scent of flowers behind.

"Do you need to go Benjamin?"

"I do."

"How much for you to stay?"

"Oh, I don't see men."

"Ok, well if you ever change your mind."

David took more money from the safe and handed it to me whilst I took down the rest of the whisky.

"There's a lot more where that came from."

"Thank you."

I handed him my glass and left before he could say goodbye, then drove down Scarlett's scented road. The flower scent grew stronger as I left the room and I soon caught her up at the lift. We didn't speak, we didn't even look at one another as the lift descended. Leaving her waiting must have been enough for her to hate me. I could even sense a hint of embarrassment. Or maybe that's what she thought I would think. And really, she was just making sure she didn't care what I thought, and that I meant nothing to her and that she still had a heart, somewhere, buried. The truth is I respected her. I couldn't imagine many women being happy to meet with two male strangers and having their choice of fantasy played out. What she did took balls. Would women doing this fifty years ago have ever imagined earning this much money by merely pretending most of it? Times change, but the judgement doesn't. Maybe she knew that. I assumed that what we had done wasn't always her situation, but it seemed even something like pretending was still distant from her goals and I took that as a sign she was on a path, doing it all by herself and not crying about it. It wasn't fair that I could do the same thing and be rewarded, but I guess that will always be the argument. I wasn't on sides anymore. I could say I was able to deal with it mentally, but she seemed stronger than me at the time. To me she had money, and she had her health. If she didn't lose character she would be a winner in my eyes, and I was routing for her. The lift opened and I gently placed my hand on her shoulder hoping she took it as a form of reassurance and support. Then we walked in different directions into the normal night.

Back between the cold walls I sat for a moment before counting out the money I had earned in the past days. It made me think about Gabby and the baby. I wanted her to have it and get anything that was needed, with some hope that it would make her feel more reassured.

[Text message]
To: Peach
Was thinking to pass by tomorrow.

[Text Message]
From: Peach
Sure, ill be in all day.

[13]

The phone alarm beeped and I rolled over and turned it off. Laying for a moment whilst my identity came together and showed me who I was. It took more time for my mind to tell me where I was going. I showered and shined my teeth, got dressed and left straight for Gabby's. I knocked and took a step back at a door I would usually open. I could already feel the tension through the walls, surrounding me like my head was in a plastic bag. Those were the times in relationships when I would really get confused. The only time I would envy others who didn't seem to have long term memories. Because even though time had passed, I could still smell her hair and recite past conversations like a favourite poem or song, but for some reason that closeness had to be played out differently. I would enter a room where her hair would be so feint it was only possible for a dog to smell. The conversations would become broken, like two foreign strangers meeting in a foreign country for the first time. I hated it. I was always more of a lover than a fighter, but when it came to fighting for love it took a lot to keep me down.

Gabby opened the door and left it ajar, walking away so instantly I couldn't even catch her eye. I struggled against the tension like it was a wind pushing through the gap she'd left in the doorway. Inside, the place felt different, cramped, even though there was one less person staying there. Even the smell was different. Have you ever had that feeling, or is it just me? The whole confusion over how you felt, like you've walked side by side with someone on this earth then suddenly it's like you are on another planet. I walked cautiously towards the living area where I could already see she had balled up on the sofa, holding her knees to her chest, a clear sign I was to sit as far away as I had expected.

"How are you?" I said, voice cracking.

"I'm good, how are you?"

"I'm ok."

"What have you been up to?" she asked, quickly scanning my body.

"Nothing," I quickly replied, instantly regretting my word of choice.

"Nothing? Have you found another job or even been looking for one?"

"Yes of course I have, that's what I meant to say. Look, I don't want to fight."

"We're not!"

"How are you feeling, have you been sick or been to the doctors?"

"I have an appointment in a few days, just to check everything is ok."

I took out most of the cash I had earned and placed it beside her. She scanned it before holding it in the air.

"Where did you get this from?"

"I borrowed it from my dad."

"Why are you giving it to me?"

"Well, I thought you could get some things for the baby, be prepared a little before I'm working again."

"This isn't enough."

"I know, I just wanted to give something for now."

[Text message]
From: London's Calling
7pm
2 HOURS
****** ROAD
Role playing

[Text message]
To: London's Calling
Role Play?

[Text message]
From: London's Calling
A few scenarios will be easy

[Text message]
To: London's Calling
Let's do it why not

"I need to go."

"Where?"

"To make more money."

"OK."

"Let me know about the appointment."

"Uh-hmm."

I left with more energy, a sudden boost formed by purpose and will, like I actually had a purpose again and was ready. There wasn't much time but enough to get home and shower and shine my teeth. After the rush I decided to take a few minutes to recompose and order a taxi. A little flush with the cash so thought why not. It felt nice to be driven where I was the only passenger; it had even been a while since I'd been in a car. I was dropped on a road where one side contained tall business buildings that towered over a long row of small symmetrical public looking houses. The houses had been converted into hotel apartments, but it was difficult to notice any signs as the area was dimly lit with gas style streetlamps. After sending in my arrival to headquarters I leant against one of the lampposts and lit up a cigarette. I noticed a full moon. It settled me for a while until I remembered I had forgotten a fuck buddy. Naturally, I started to worry, as I would have no encouragement if both the physical and mental attraction were a miss. I continued to look at the moon. The orange tone was hypnotic and relaxing. I began stretching my neck out and blowing nicotine like a howling wolf, sending any worry up into clouds of smoke. I stubbed the cigarette out with my shoe as I noticed someone exit one of the public houses and make their way in my direction. As they came closer I noticed a woman in her mid-forties, above average on the weight side with long shiny hair that lit more of the street than the lamps. Her weight wasn't the only thing above average. The closer she came, the taller she looked. Appealing long legs that played a part in portraying an unfavourable attitude. A strong thrust of the hips at each stride, the road becoming her catwalk. Once she reached me she towered over me just like the business buildings over the houses. She was wearing a leather skirt, a leather jacket and leather boots, finished off with leather bracelets. Close up, her weight was more thick than oversized. She had daunting eyes and a strong accent, making her somewhat intimidating, escorted by a drug-fuelled slur.

"You are quite short," she said with a plain expression.

"Yes! Well I could spend the rest of my life worrying or see the positives."

"What are the positives?"

"Well, I was cursed with short legs but blessed with three."

"You could be tall and still be well endowed."

"I could, but there could always be something else effective or replaced."

"Like what?"

"Rhythm or knowing how to please."

"Ok, so there are people tall, well endowed, and know how to please."

"And the list would go on. Money, intelligence, a matching sense of humor. The whole reason no one is perfect is because the list of perfection is endless and to even match two on that list is rare."

Her lips sided for a smudge second. If you blinked or weren't looking at her mouth at the moment you would have missed it, a smidge of a smirk. She wanted to smile but I guess she felt more comfortable playing a model.

"Follow me," she said whilst spinning around.

Which caused the bottom of her hair to swipe across my face, a subtle slap. Returning up the platform, I followed like an unworthy competitor in her ten-foot shadow. Once we reached the houses, I couldn't help but notice it was not the one she'd come out from. A group of hotel staff were smoking close to where we were trying to enter. I could feel their eyes all over us. Although more so on her as she was fighting with a door she clearly didn't have a key for. After the tenth round, she decided to throw in the towel and ask for assistance from the smokers. One quickly perked up, looked at the key and pointed to the apartment three doors down, the original building she'd come from. As we made our way, she shifted her frustration onto me.

"Why were you late?"

"Sorry, I lost track of time."

I wasn't late. In fact, I was ten minutes early, but I didn't want to get into that. I thought for certain then, and more so without my fuck buddy, that I was in for a challenging evening. When we reached the room, the model collapsed on the bed after pointing out some cash and a large white mountain of snow on the dresser. She said I was to help myself. I stood awkwardly for a moment as she lay on the bed. Assuming at first it was from exhaustion after going ten rounds with a door and she just wanted a rest, it began to look more like she had slipped into a coma. The room was very small and dark apart from one lamp on the dresser, which only lit the top of the table, highlighting the cash and powder and some sheets of paper.

I walked over to the dresser and pocketed the cash before taking a credit card from my wallet and playing with the snow. I finished making ten evenly spread lines but didn't stop there; I took a note from my pocket and rolled it up. I then halved one of the lines, as I didn't want to carry full guilt, as I was well aware of the rates and knew I was about to waste it. I leant forward and placed the note to my nose, blowing the substance away instead of sniffing it. The blowing had alarmed the comatose and she appeared from nowhere, like a cat's bowl you accidentally kick. She sniffed three of the ten lines in one go.

After her go on the slopes, she slipped off her boots and skirt and removed her jacket, falling back onto the bed face down like she had just woken in the night to empty her bladder before lunging back into deep sleep. I had always heard the substance kept you awake, which always kept me away. But it seemed to have the opposite effect on her. Maybe being a catwalk model she was just playing hard to get, or maybe it was part of the role-play, who knew. She was only wearing what I thought was a thong at first but as I stepped closer I noticed it was actually a pair of granny panties her large cheeks had chewed all the way into her crack. If it wasn't for the cinematic lighting and my photographic eye I'm almost certain I would have made a run for it. I moved over to a different point on the opposite side of the bed where I spotted one large breast sticking out, the other hidden under her slanted positioning. It was typical really, and just my luck, the first time I forgot my fuck buddy was when I was in need of him most. As I contemplated how to address the matter,

143

she suddenly jumped out of her state, brushed passed me and grabbed two sheets of paper from the dresser. She then flung one into my stomach and held onto the other before perching on the bed facing me as if we'd been conversing all evening. It was the most uncomfortable stare-off in the history of stare-offs. She just stared like a tipsy toad awaiting some kind of answer or action, and I was staring back at a tipsy toad trying to figure out what the fuck had just happened. It wasn't long, but felt like a whole night. It finally hit me when she said:

"Just read it as naturally as you can. Don't think too much."

I looked down and scanned the piece of paper. It contained half a page of text in a script-like format with separated MALE and FEMALE sections, with the constant use of double letters as if the keys had stuck. I took a step back and read the title 'GOOD COP BAD GIRL'. I took a breath and began reading:

[MALE]
"So Doreen, Iff thaat is your reeal name. Looking over at your statementt, I discoveredd you either have the capability of being in two places at once or you've been telling porkies. Now. I won't beeat around the bush that's not my style, imm a straight in kind of guy and right noww I don't have the time. It's anal Wednesday at my house and the wife will be very, very disappointed if I'm not back, so tell me have you been a bad girl?"

I glanced up from the script. She was still in the same-perched position on the edge of the bed. Although she held a different expression on her face from when I had last looked. She was no longer intimidating, no smidge smirks, just subtle seductive movements from the lips, and a flirtatious stare, a whole different woman. She didn't read from her paper either; she didn't even have the paper in her hands, it was nowhere to be seen. What struck me were the handcuffs she had wrapped around her wrists and her chest pushed right out.

[FEMALE]
"You have a wife?"

Her acting was very good. Few words but convincing, so much so I actually wondered if she'd really asked me if I had a wife. I paused for a moment, unsure how to respond before remembering it was part of the play. I had the reply in my hand.

[MALE]
"Yes, I have a wife. A loving loyal and doting wife in fact. Why do you ask, do that..."

"Oh Sorry." I broke character for a second.

[MALE]
"...DOES that surprise you?"

[FEMALE]
"No not at all. You are very handsome, it's just. Well, it's just a shame."

[MALE]
"How so?"

[FEMALE]
"Well, because with me it could be anal Wednesday every day."

The script directed I take a sip of water, which I didn't have. She had forgotten to provide the rest of the props, so I quickly improvised and took out my rolled note and once again performed my little nose-blowing trick with one of the lines on the dresser. This excited her and she pushed her chest out even further.

[MALE]
"Mrs. white! You have been arrested on the suspicion of murder, the murder of your husband."

[FEMALE]
"My husband is dead?"

[MALE]
"Yes!"

[FEMALE]
"Well then I guess he will never find out about us will he!"

She then jumped up from the bed and grabbed me with her cuffed grip. We were only a breast's width apart before she pushed them onto me. She then lent down and we began passionately kissing. I don't know if it was the kiss or the role-play or both, but it was only seconds until I had matched our distance by the waist down. My batten had drawn itself and she quickly dropped down onto her knees after feeling it push onto her and began polishing it.

After a few moments, she broke character, stood up and made her way over to the corner where she began rummaging in a plastic carry bag. She removed a garment and threw it my way.

"Put this on."

146

It turned out to be a pair of blue overalls, oversized at that. I put them on, unsure of the next act to come, feeling like a young lad that had on his dads hand me downs. She sniffed a line from the dresser and leafed through more sheets of paper on the dresser before handing me another. As I scanned the text she played around with the bed cover, folding half and pulling it back so the bed sheet became visible. She arched over inspecting it, her arms crossed behind her back.

[FEMALE]
"I just don't understand I only bought the thing a month ago."

I looked down at my new script. We were back to it again.

[MALE]
"You can never be too sure about these things. Engines are like men Mrs Richards. Some work longer than others but eventually, they all let you down."

She began laughing hysterically, rolling her head around and throwing her hair back several times before moving closer and placing the palm of her hand onto my chest.

[FEMALE]
"Is there anything you can do, you know to get my engine running again?"

[MALE]
"I know a thing or two about getting an engine running yes, but it's a lot of HARD work."

She then looked down at the bedsheet and pretended to play around with the invisible car components.

[FEMALE]
"Maybe it's this?"
[MALE]
"That's just a dipstick."
[FEMALE]
"Ooh a dick stick!"
[MALE]
"No a dip stick Mrs. Richards, di-P..."
[FEMALE]
"Oh, what does a diP-stick do?"
[MALE]
"Its there to check if the oil needs filling up."
[FEMALE]
"Does it need filling up?"
[MALE]
"I would need to dip it and check."
[FEMALE]
"yes dip it in"

She moved closer to me, touching me with both hands and pushing me up against the bottom of the bed frame where again she dropped to her knees and undid the fly on the overalls and began sucking. As I started to relax and enjoy it she jumped up, and again rummaged through the plastic bag in the corner, taking another garment and walking toward the en suite.

"Wait here."

She closed the door behind her and I stood there thumb twiddling, which went on for a good five minutes. I ran through the obvious kinds of character who might emerge, and what role I would be taking on. Many scenarios came to mind. Priest and confessor, lawyer and defendant, bodyguard and politician. The bathroom door finally opened but I didn't see anything; I could only hear an absurd panting sound. After a long minute, she began crawling out on all fours, dressed in a brown one-piece fur outfit with a hood that had ears sewn on. She crawled over to me and began rubbing her head against my leg, spinning around to display a large hole cut out from the outfit around the back area.

"WOOF WOOF"

I didn't know what to do. There was no A4 sheet of paper this time. And really it might have been more appropriate if she'd played a cat because something certainly held my tongue. Unable to think of anything to say I finally reached out to pat her.

"WOOF"

She then turned and showed her rear to me, looking over her shoulder and barking some more, encouraging me to play along. I took a condom from my pocket and held it up and began to play master.

"Would you like a treat?"

"Woof!"

I separated the rubber from the plastic and knelt down, holding the wrapper out in the palm of my hand. She took it with her mouth and began throwing it around the room and jumping on it.

"Woof Woof Woof"

I removed the oversized overalls and finished putting on the condom as she looked back before sticking up her bum and leaning on to her elbows. I approached and squatted down slightly, holding a piece of the fur cut out to one side, performing quite literally the doggy style position. With each slow thrust there was a crying sound. I continued at the same pace but the cry's soon stopped and the barks returned.

"What do you want?"

"Woooooof!"

"Harder? Faster?"

"Woof Woof Woof!"

I sped up with harder thrusts and the cries returned. I could feel her tensing up and I continued in the same spot as she made a repetitive cry until finally she filled the room.

"OWOOOOOOOOOOOOOOOOO"

As she howled, I picked up the pace even more as I could feel I was close. It wasn't long until I joined in, closing my eyes and stretching my neck up.

"OWOOOOOOOOOOOOOOOOO"

I opened my eyes and noticed the orange-tinted full moon through the window, which made me produce another howl.

"OWOOOOOOOOOOOOOOOOO"

My howling set the model off and she also produced another.

"OWOOOOOOOOOOOOOOOOO"

The howling stopped. I remained squatting a moment as she began panting, slowly falling flat onto the floor and releasing me. I stood up and watched over her for a moment before getting dressed, patting her on the head and leaving the room for one where I felt more normal.

[14]

I stood amongst another chaos, but with a home-like feeling. Three visits in four days. I felt a part of the place, a cog in the roulette wheel. I even received a couple of head nods from the dealers as I made my over to a table. When I found a spot, I took out my weekly earnings, plus my weekly winnings, and placed half down on the table to exchange for the plastic. Nothing was new to me except the fresh-faced dealer, so fresh it was still all red. I caught a passing waitress and ordered a drink before the first hand, only to turn back to the dealer already making twenty-one. Beginner's luck, I thought. Which in fact turned out to be just the beginning. Honestly, I couldn't have written it if I tried. Three twenty ones in a row, and not even from aces or picture cards. He made twenty-one starting with a six and even a three. The more I lost, the more I doubled the plastic on the table, casting deeper into my pockets for the other half of my money. Before I could count to twenty-one, I was cleaned out. Not exactly everything; walking away with some beer coupons would be the right move, but the majority was certainly gone. I'd gone into it feeling like nothing was new, but this certainly was. Around two and a half thousand spent before a ten-pound drink was poured and served. I made my way to the exit but not before stopping and looking to see if Alexandra or Stacey and Lacy were around. Of course, they weren't. Like the easy money I'd been handed, the universe continued to take away everything else. The money, the girls, then hope, a little of the hope anyway, which was kind enough to escort me from the building then left me by myself once outside. I was back with only the company of a dark cloud, all the weight back on my head, my view of the buildings blocked, as were the lights and the people who passed. I was broke, miserable and worst of all sober.

I stopped dragging my feet and managed to pick my head up to look round. I was back to where it all began. I entered the first pub I saw, ordered the first beer I'd tried as a teen when I'd sat at the bar for the first time on my own. Everything was slower. I was able to observe as opposed to playing my usual role amongst friends. I watched for some time, having a few beers and the odd tequila. Noticing a unique environment where the rich converse with the poor, the educated with those who never went to school, con men and their targets, many minor differences but one major similarity. Moving around like chess pieces discussing the complexities of life and their next move, alcohol numbing the heartache as well as providing false inspiration to escape a checkmate impression. It felt like school. Where even a bell would ring after the lesson was finished. Instead of rushing out, everyone begged to stay.

I overheard parts of a discussion I was all too familiar with, coming from over my shoulder. A group of young lads. Two were carrying the conversation as the other two sat back, finding it somewhat tiresome but agreeing, so I'm sure they had been there at some point themselves. The two on good terms wanted to be good friends so of course continued to drink, just at a slower rate, encouraged to enjoy themselves. Not knowing, after strolling back home when the cocks are crowing, would not hold well with the chick. They would more than likely become the keynote speakers the following meet up.

One of the talkers then held out his phone, which I assumed displayed an attractive person as certain remarks followed, moving from reality into fantasy for a few minutes. The main proposal is that the two gulpers provided self-hope and projected options to sustain pride. Just like most of us have done at some point. We've complained or even shoved hate towards someone we know and shared a life with, then spoken highly about those we've never met. I'm sure Madonna and Mr Bond have been used in that consequence many a time, just like the popular star of their decade everyone speaks of. I felt it was because one can create a list, the physical and status already flatter and we can then simply apply genuine desire with the power of our imagination to self-suit and play out the behavioural traits we feel our partner should hold. Then, as we get older, we begin reminiscing and missing the puppy love days where only purity laid, and money, material items and titles were just for the full-grown dogs. Forced teachings just like school, and realising when it's too late, or more likely forgotten, and wherever there are rules there is a game.

The Love Game

Have a go at spreading your wings and taking flight by becoming a lovebird. A two-player game that has its up. Each player will create a list. A list that is usually developed from your memories in experiencing stories that go back to Shakespeare and modern film, combined with personal experiences with parents, family and friends. Favourite foods and films, music and the games you played as kids, followed by dream destinations and furthermore romantic gestures involving flowers and jewellery. Once you have crafted your particular list of checkboxes both players will then try to tick off and match as many of these boxes with the other player. You will soon come to realise as the boxes are checked off, laughter will grow and the time shared together also grows and in more time love is made and made and made. Your wings will flourish and you can take flight and share the freedom-like sensation with your partner along with the exchanging promise of never ending-up like one another's parents and will continue to love one another unconditionally forever happily after.

We shall not be held accountable/responsible if the players continue to play past the recommended game length and or try to force their partner to tick off boxes. Players may experience disagreement as the game goes on. A battle as such on whose vision of love is the right vision, whose definition of loyalty and trust is correct, how caring should be expressed, physical preferences and sexual fulfilments and furthermore timing for children and marriage. Players may experience difficulty trying to keep flight as a couple alongside working on self-goals and the many other UN shared dreams. This can lead to experiencing a period of time where the boxes are no longer being checked off. Laughter becomes the odd grin, the time-shared becomes separate and in more time our competitors' game Hate is played and played and played. Your wings will lose strength and you will fall closer to captivity each day until finally you land in your parent's shoes and continue their footsteps forever unhappily after.

[Text Message]
From: London's Calling
Are you still in the city?

[Text message]
To: London's Calling
Yes

[Text Message]
From: London's Calling
Single lady enquiry

[Text Message]
To: London's Calling
The same one?

[Text Message]
From: London's Calling
No

[Text Message]
To: London's Calling
Ok

[Text Message]
From: London's Calling
***** **** Hotel
Room 22

[Text Message]
To: London's Calling
Let me check

[Text Message]
From: London's Calling
Ok

[Text Message]
To: London's Calling
I can be there in twenty minutes

[Text Message]
From: London's Calling
Great I will let her know

And so it seemed when one casino door closed a door
to a hotel room opened.

I turned up at the hotel somewhat over the limit; one further sip would occasion a visit from the drop phase. I wasn't too sure about attending the meet at all as I could barely walk. It wasn't exactly like my old job where I could sit at my desk and pretend to work. The only thought to persuade me was to show I was there for Gabby. So I entered through the large glass doors to a basic lobby, not as nice as the previous places, only the kind of hotel you would take someone during the exploring stages, when you didn't care to impress. Cheap golden tiles covered the flooring like a desert. The few plants had been scattered round obscurely, filling the air with a rich scent of aloe Vera. It didn't even feel like the same country. I made my way to the lift, looking out for any other sign of life. Everything was in slow motion. I felt like I had two heads moving from side to side, trying to sync back into one. I eventually passed a large wooden reception desk with just one clerk. I smiled, nodded, held up my arm and waved to avoid any suspicion. It must have worked as he quickly looked away and went back to filing some paperwork.

I entered the lift and pushed for the floor. As the doors closed, I was overcome by a psychic inkling, like when a stranger you often see in the local supermarket comes to mind and then, a few minutes later, you actually see them somewhere else. No one specific came to mind but the feeling lingered. On the third floor I stood staring at a gold plaque on the wall indicating directions and door numbers. I really tried to remember but I couldn't. I took my phone out of my pocket to remind myself before wobbling my way to the room. The corridors were like a maze and the number of doors I walked through seemed unnecessary. Before I could work out where I was, I realised I was right back to where I wasn't meant to be. Staring at the same gold plaque on the wall just outside the lift. I recomposed and took a deep breath, rechecked my phone for the room number and followed the direction in which the plaque suggested, that time with less wobble in my stride. Several turns and several fire doors later I managed to find room 22 or 222. It blurred between the two, and I knocked and shakily waited.

The door swiftly opened and a lady moved even quicker to the bathroom, just beside the entry. I could only catch a glimpse of her dark hair. I entered and closed the door just as she closed the bathroom door.

"I won't be long. There's some wine on the table, help yourself."

"Thank you."

I walked further into the room toward the bottle, like a moth to a flame, or to be more accurate, like an alcoholic to a bottle of wine.

"There's only a little bit left are you sure I can have it?" I asked whilst pouring it into the glass.

"It's fine," a high-pitched response echoed from the bathroom.

I took a couple of steps towards the bed and perched on the end and began sipping. A few sips in, the toilet flushed and the bathroom door opened. A lady in her late twenties approached me.

"Hello, sorry about that. As you can see, I had a bit to drink already and it's just starting to escape."

"That's fine. Sorry I had the last bit," I said whilst holding up the glass.

"Well…"

She quickly rushed to her bag in the corner and pulled out another bottle.

"I came prepared!" she said, pouring out a large glass for herself.

She was very bubbly, and couldn't seem to stand still; it was almost like she had a bounce in her step even when she didn't move. She was well spoken and had a sense of professionalism, a woman who knew what she wanted.

"So it's Benjamin right?"

"Yes."

"I'm Imogen."

"Nice to meet you, Imogen."

She joined me at the edge of the bed and we clinked glasses.

"Nice to meet you too."

A sudden thumping at the door grabbed our tongues. She looked at me wide eyed and I frowned back in confusion, my heart imitating the pace of the knock. We both looked over at the door and then back at one another again before Imogen remembered.

"Oh, I ordered snacks."

She ran over to open the door and took a tray from the staff member, then walked back and placed it onto the table next to the wine.

"Just some olives and nuts, in case we got peckish," she continued.

"Good thinking," I replied with a smirk.

"Oh, I brought some oil too. Would you kindly give me a massage?"

"Yeah, sure."

"Great."

"You've really come prepared, have you done this before?"

"Hahahaha. No No it's my first time, I think you met my boss and his wife"

"Always nervous looking?"

"Yes that's them"

"I see"

"I'm quite close to her and she told me about it and so I thought, why not"

"Very well"

She walked over to her neatly arranged corner of bags again and took out a small bottle of oil.

"So this is for you," she said, handing me the oil.

She then re-approached her corner and took out an envelope of money and handed it to me.

"And this is also for you."

I placed the oil down on the bed and took the envelope.

"Thank you, and thank you," I replied as I nodded at the oil and held up the envelope.

She finished off her glass of wine and slipped of her dress. It fell to her feet. She remained standing in her underwear.

"I'm ready when you are," she said with a slight giggle.

And she jumped onto the bed face down. She really was ready. I stood up, finished my drink and placed my glass next to hers on the table before removing my shoes and collecting the oil, crouching over her lower back.

"Is it ok if I remove this," I asked, tugging on her bra strap.

"Yes," she said, muffled within the pillow.

I removed her strap and began applying the oil, followed by gentle rubs with the palms of my hands up and down her back. I had witnessed a giant rubber cock called Tiger, European spanking wooden panels, and even howled within a two-dog pack, but for some reason this one felt the weirdest. I applied more oil onto her legs and ran my hands all over her body. I couldn't help but think about the café where I had met George, where I entered like the familiar white mug only to be transformed, leaving as something unfamiliar. After a while everything became thoughtless. I removed her underwear slowly as I hadn't asked that time, but the pace made room for an unspoken agreement. As I removed them she rolled over and began kissing me, which surpassed any more needed reassurance. She began unbuttoning my shirt as we continued to kiss before moving me into her position and applying some oil to my chest. She then removed my jeans and climbed on top of me and began moving at a slow pace. Genuine desire followed, or at least relatable emotions crossing paths to make us feel that way. She was on top of me for no longer than five minutes before we had locked eyes for a moment, then both closed them whilst climaxing together. She climbed off and no words were exchanged for a moment until that special part of us that separates us from the animal kingdom returned.

"I didn't wear any protection."

"Oh that's fine I'm taking birth control."

She dressed and tied her hair up before approaching her tidy corner of bags one final time.

"So, I have to go, but you don't have to rush."

"OK," I replied with a slight frown.

"If you can just drop off the key cards to the desk, that will be great."

"Sure."

"They are…. There." She pointed them out on the desk

162

"Ok," I replied whist looking over at the cards.

"Byeeeeeee," she said nervously.

She didn't look me in the eye or even come near me, she just left in her bouncy step and I was left with half a bottle of wine, some olives and nuts and my thoughts.

I got up and walked over to the wine. I didn't even get dressed. I just poured some more into my glass before taking my phone out from my jeans on the bed and sat in the chair next to the table and began sipping.

[Text message]
From: Soft Bonner
Wheer'e r you?

[Text message]
From: Soft Bonner
The girls herey are amaze inn

[Text message]
From: Soft Bonner
Are you coming?

After realising I had nowhere to rush off to, all I remember is feeling the company of the drop phase. Which was strange, as I also remember looking over at the bottle of wine in that moment, to check the strength. Instead, I noticed the clear, bold letters under the branding: NON-ALCOHOLIC. Next thing, I found myself standing on the hotel roof, looking over what should have been a familiar city. It felt more like a foreign land instead, and I was merely a visitor. I looked up at an empty night sky where the weight fell back onto my shoulders. Attacked by the aggressive cold wind, I struggled to stand and keep my balance as it pushed. My favourite song wasn't playing, only the violent sound of the wind, each gust forcing me that little bit closer to the edge. I looked down but couldn't quite make out anything, a darkened blur, my heart racing as I knew that only one more visit from the wind would bring it all into focus.

[Text message]
From: Peach
Could you pass by tomorrow, need to see you

I took a deep breath and struggled a while, trying to find my feet which were the last thing I remembered seeing, followed by the sound of a door closing.

[15]

I woke that morning like a zombie on the night of Halloween, my phone no longer shaking me up. I must have finally turned off the alarm. There was no staring at the ceiling or identity piecing. I knew who I was. There was no care in recollecting the previous days; I was thinking more of the future. I showered and shined my teeth and got dressed and left straight for Gabby's. This time when I knocked, she opened the door and stood aside. We didn't speak until we were in the living area. I noticed she was still wearing a patient band around her wrist and I felt my stomach shoot right up to my throat.

"Everything Ok?" I asked nervously.

And Gabby began crying. Answering my question with action not words and I understood completely what she was saying. I moved over to offer my shoulder for her head, holding her with both arms, which only squeezed a deeper cry.

"It's ok, what happened?"

After a few minutes the tears had stopped, the air was replaced in her lungs. She removed her head from my shoulders.

"I had some pains last night for hours, I thought it was normal until I started having some discharge which had a little blood in and I went to the hospital and that's when they told me."

"Told you what?"

"A miscarriage," she said, now sobbing.

I'd already expected the worst after seeing her patient band. Hearing the words was something else. It made hearing a girlfriend in your teens telling you she wanted to be friends comical. I felt like I had been placed on the tallest mountain in the deepest ocean where going anywhere, in any direction, was impossible. Removing every drop of strength from your body knowing you could do nothing but stand still and take it. Every time I tried to speak, Gabby's tears soaked up my words and my mouth would close. Gabby rose and left the living room only to return with the cash I had given her and the last words I would ever hear from her.

"I don't want to continue this anymore."

[Text message]
From: London's Calling
Able to meet for the commission today?

[Text message]
To: London's Calling
Yeah where?

[Text message]
From: London's Calling
Same Café say one hour?

[Text message]
To: London's Calling
Ok

I left the apartment and made my way to the train station at a fast pace whilst chugging down some nicotine.

Rushing to go nowhere. I entered the same clustered cafe as before except this time I was late. George was already sitting in the corner stirring his espresso, a concerned look on his face as I approached. He stood once I reached him and we shook hands and sat opposite one another again, on a table with a manikin head placed in the middle.

"Good to see you Benjamin, would you like anything?"

"No I'm fine," I replied.

"So…. having fun? How are you finding everything?"

"Tiring."

"Hahahaha yes. London's Calling baby."

And just like that his smile was back and I could tell right then that we were going to have some differences, but I no longer cared. I felt I could no longer do right. The harder I tried, the more it had the opposite effect. I had to start thinking about what was right for me, I just hoped it wouldn't go on for too long. George seemed like the guy who could sell the shed skin back to a snake, or at least the snake would buy it just to shut him up.

"I met Sonya a few times. She was crazy right?"

"Sonya?"

"The lady, wild one, with all her papers and costumes."

"Oh, I didn't catch her name."

"Yes Sonya. I think. One time we were in a hotel with, how you say, spa. Jacuzzi and a big pool. She wanted to be dolphin. She was doing the noise, you know, click click click."

I took the cash from my pocket and placed it on the table and slid it toward him.

"It's been a good week yes?" he said whilst counting the cash

"I can't do this anymore."

The concerned look was back. George reclined in the chair with a subtle smirk on his face and bounced his head up and down slowly before continuing his sales pitch.

"I think you are not thinking. This is just the beginning, what else are you going to do?"

"I have some things I wish to pursue."

"What things?"

"Other work that is more suiting to me."

"Trust me. You will regret so much and it's only just beginning, this is every man's dream."

"If it's every man's dream, then you won't have any problem finding new people."

"It may be every man's dream but to most men, it will stay a dream. There are certain things. Reliability, trust. Being able to do handle the Sonya's of this world. Not

168

many can do that. Most can't even get it up when they need to."

"I'm sorry".

"Ok. Why don't you just take a few days off, and then we can meet."

"I don't want to give false hope."

"After a few days, you may see things different."

"I won't."

I held a look of seriousness in my eyes and George finally gave up, still holding the snakeskin. He stood when I did, a false smirk, a nod of his head whilst holding out his hand. We shook.

Once back in the shop flat it felt like the earth had stopped spinning, maybe because I shut myself off from the world and spent most of the time staring at an un-opened bottle of vodka. Many frowns and smiles occurred during the stare as I hopped the fine line between love and hate. Something I had always looked at for answers, but which only ever produced more questions. My knowledge went down with the liquid. I didn't have a single sip, the power of control had shifted, and I was no longer telling myself that it was me in control. Rather, it was me being controlled, and for some reason I didn't like that feeling. Hearing Gabby say she no longer wanted to continue made me realise I had come to the end and lost everything. I no longer wanted to continue that path, that direction. Not drinking alcohol allowed me to separate feeling from thought, reality from fantasy, and happiness from expectation. I realised I am not responsible for anyone else's happiness, but more importantly they are not responsible for mine. I wasn't ready to care for a child despite how I felt, but that's what alcohol does. It makes you feel you can do anything, whilst everyone around you sees someone who can do nothing. Working on yourself so you can eventually attract people who do the same, so there is nothing but sharing happiness instead of trying to create it.

It takes time, but with each day you begin to see clearer, you begin to feel what you really want, you become who you really are. There may be no meaning to life but the one you give. A story, with a beginning, middle and an end, and the people you meet are characters, all of which create moments, memories, a dream-like feeling that makes you want more and more to continue and enjoy this mysterious and wonderful existence. Going from too many hours in the day to being motivated, inspired and realising there are not enough hours. That to me is pure. That to me is purpose.

A few months passed, felt like a year. It was the beginning of the week. Monday morning. My phone alarm beeped, I hit the off button on my phone and rolled straight out of bed to shower and shine my teeth. I got half-dressed in the bedroom and then headed to the kitchen to make some breakfast, after which I put on my ironed shirt that was hanging up waiting for me.

I stood outside, looking up for a minute, appreciative of the building I was happy to be away from home in. A projection of warmth no matter the weather. Smooth sliding doors that welcomed me into a bright sun-filled reception. I headed for the elevator and pushed for the fourth floor. A smooth ride that gracefully carried me to a room displaying fresh walls, tidy desks and a fifteen-litre water cooler with endless amounts of plastic cups.

I then headed to Peter's office, my boss's office. He always insisted you called him by his first name, so much so that for the first two months I didn't even know what his family name was. We never socialised out of work, but we'd certainly built a relationship. I knocked on his door and entered the room.

"Mr early, I'm starting to think you sleep here."

"Morning Peter."

I sat down in a comfortable chair opposite Peter's large oak wood desk.

"Did you do anything nice at the weekend?"

"Nothing much to be honest. Just relaxed. And you?"

"Played some tennis with my wife."

"Did she beat you again?"

"Yes, she did actually. So the Mediterranean food bill was on me that night. And then Sunday, just relaxed at home, the weather was nice so we just sat in the garden."

"Yes, it was lovely."

"How is the content going for the jewellery client?"

"I'll be done with that today."

"Great. Well, I wanted to see you as I'm very happy with your work, even more happy with your punctuality and so wanted to let you know that the intern period is over and there is a position for you to stay, if you want it of course."

"Of course. Thank you."

"Great, I will get all the paperwork over to you this afternoon."

"Great, thanks again."

"Welcome."

I would usually take something in to eat, as often I would continue to work during my lunch hour, avoiding the stampede of people in the city. That day I was little rushed, so I had to step out and visit the local supermarket. The only problem I had that day was the choice of sandwiches. I actually think if I hadn't been spoilt for choice I wouldn't have been standing there indecisively for five minutes, and he would never have spotted me.

"I wouldn't eat here, you'll get food poisoning."

I turned to see Paul in his high visibility jacket and hardhat, leaving a road of sand from his boots as he approached me.

"Why are you here?" he continued

"I have a new job, not too far from here. Why you are here?" I replied.

"I'm working on a new build in the area and I'm meeting Emma for lunch."

"That's nice."

"Emma!" Paul shouted out over my shoulder.

"There she is," Paul continued.

I turned and noticed a girl walking towards us with bright eyes and a huge smile on her face. I had never met Emma before that moment. But under the name Imogen I had. Watching her approach was like slow motion, the blood in my body getting warmer, the hairs on my neck becoming longer the closer she came. She then took her gaze away from Paul and placed it on to me. Her eyes became dull, her smile faded. I looked down to her tummy and turned to face Paul. He'd adopted her bright eyes and huge smile whilst gently nodding his head because he noticed me clocking her baby bump.

"Babe, this is an old school friend."

"Hello," I said, as I awkwardly held out my hand.

"Hi," Emma replied, softly shaking my hand.

I couldn't take my eyes away from her stomach. We locked eyes one more time whilst I held a confused frown on my face, which Emma had spotted and seemed startled by.

"I just need to grab one more thing babe."

"Oh I couldn't find the non-alcoholic wine." Paul snapped out.

"Ok I will grab it, I'll meet you outside," she said quickly.

"Ok see you in a bit," Paul agreed.

"Bye," she said softly at me.

"Bye," I replied even softer.

Emma quickly walked away. I couldn't help but watch.

"Well what do you say?" Paul shouted.

"What?" I said with puzzled face.

"Aren't you going to say congratulations?"

"What happened? How?"

"I think it was just the pressure and overthinking, but we got back together a few days after we went out actually. Oh I'm sorry about how I was that night.."

"A few days after we went out?" I interrupted.

"Yeah."

"How many days?"

"I don't know three of four days why?"

"So no IVF?"

"Nope, we wanted to wait before trying that again as we needed the money to move"

"Move! Move where?"

"Australia, I told you, no?"

"No."

"Yeah I got a job offer; the pay is way better out there."

"What about Emma's job?"

"The company she is with here basically started in Auz. She's really close with her bosses wife, they helped her a lot"

"When are you moving?"

"Next month."

"Oh."

"I know. Listen I have to go, but we'll meet up before I go Ok?"

"Sure."

"I was only joking about the sandwiches here too. They are actually really nice. Laters."

"Later."

We clapped hands and touched shoulders one more time. Paul walked away. I watched him go. We never did meet up before he left.

END.

Milton Keynes UK
Ingram Content Group UK Ltd.
UKHW020933220724
445981UK00001B/54

9 781917 293341